THE WONDERFUL GARDEN

BY THE SAME AUTHOR

The Powers On High
(New Authors Limited)

THE
WONDERFUL GARDEN

Sylvia Bruce

 Hutchinson of London

HUTCHINSON & CO (Publishers) LTD
178–202 Great Portland Street, London W1

London Melbourne Sydney
Auckland Bombay Toronto
Johannesburg New York

First published 1969

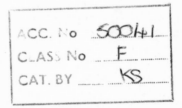

This book has been set in Pilgrim, printed in Great Britain
on Antique Wove paper by Anchor Press, and
bound by Wm. Brendon, both of Tiptree, Essex

09 098140 5

For Margaret Eastman
and for Paddy Owens

Duologue one

'I do wish good people weren't so boring,' she said crossly, emptying, with disgust, the most repellent of the ash-trays. 'Try behind the curtains, Paul, there must be at least a dozen more glasses somewhere.'

The search completed, 'I caught a snatch of what you were saying about St Joan,' he remarked. 'Is she the kind of person you call good?'

'St Joan? No,' Anne said decidedly. 'I don't think she was good at all—she was so consciously virtuous, so fanatical!'

He remonstrated. 'You can't dismiss as mere fanaticism everything you dislike.'

'There's nothing "mere" about fanaticism.' She stacked the dishes. 'It creates most of the world's history and all its trouble: Hitler, Christ, Casanova. . . . As for St Joan, even if watching her undrape didn't excite the French troops, I bet their presence at her toilet gave *her* a kick!'

'You're capable of quite astounding vileness,' Paul commented.

Shaken, perhaps by her own words rather than by his, at first she said nothing. Then she burst out: 'Why is it that those who've devoted their lives to defloration have such a sickly respect for virginity?'

'Don't be absurd,' he said. 'I had very few affairs before meeting you, and since then ...'

'Why do they always say *women* take everything personally?' she interrupted.

'You *meant* it personally, as you very well know.'

'Paul, Paul,' she said tiredly. 'Why do we always end up like this? Perhaps' (she tried to be dispassionate, and, as usual, the effort brought her to the brink of tears) 'I did exaggerate, but I only meant St Joan was as far as it's possible to be from my concept of goodness. She was one of the guilt-causing ones, she brought no peace!'

'With your liking for heretics,' said Paul, 'you should thoroughly approve of her.'

'No, because she felt so sure of being right, just like those who burned her. Reverse their positions ...' She picked up the mop.

'But if she *was* right? After all, in the end she was canonised!'

'The good are never canonised; that's exactly what I mean. You don't have three-star water, do you?'

'Well, who *is* good, then?' he demanded, his irritation already immense.

'Happy people, I suppose,' she replied, musing. 'The Farmers, for instance: Celia, and half-wit brother Roddy. You could put both of them in a perfectly mad-driving situation and they wouldn't notice it was there.'

'Oh, come!' he protested. 'That's not true. People aren't, are they, good, or happy, all in one go? You talk as though the Farmers had no problems, no temptations, but that's not fair to them.'

'Temptations? Why do you say that? Still, it may be the crux. I'm sure the temptations of good people *are* weaker than ours.'

'There's nothing particularly strong about mine,' he said, resisting the attempt at conspiracy.

'Then why,' she retorted, 'do you yield to them so often?

Your urge to contradict everything I say—isn't that a temptation, and a strong one?'

'It's a moot point who does the contradicting. I only meant that my temptations are much weaker than I should imagine Celia's, for instance, are,'

'Celia?' She laughed. 'She's as innocent as a baby.'

He shook his head. 'Celia's very nearly a saint.'

'She's certainly as boring as one!'

'You know so *little* about her!' Paul exclaimed.

'Which of us has known her the longer?'

'There's very little connexion between time and understanding. You call *Celia* happy?'

'You're very touchy on her behalf,' Anne observed. 'If *she's* not happy, who is?'

'I can tell you who else is *not*, and that's Roderick!'

She stared, incredulous. 'If there's anyone who's incapable of being anything *but* happy, it's Roderick.'

'Do you have to be articulate to feel pain?'

'Language and ideas are so closely connected, I don't see how you could be called conscious of any mental pain if you couldn't evoke it or describe it,' Anne said thoughtfully, swirling the dishes round. 'I suppose you'd have to be capable of expression before you could respond to a dazzling happiness too, but on a lower level, just the absence of pain, surely the Farmers are happy? They seem horribly contented, at least.'

'For heaven's sake, Anne, let's leave this. It grates on me, somehow.'

Yet it was he who, a moment later, returned to it. 'Very few people are able to experience happiness at a high level, to my mind. I can think of only two others, as a matter of fact, who are even contented, and they—oh, they belonged to another age!'

Her curiosity was aroused.

'You didn't know them,' Paul said. 'They were the owners of a house I stayed at, a long time ago. I'll always remember it: the utter peace. Roses; a cool, sharp, good smell when you entered the kitchen from their wonderful garden—redcurrants or something—and a red tiled floor. Not the same red as the currants, though—orange, rather, with a warm gloss of age, or care. And home-made wine and marmalades—and sunshine, always, all the time I was with them. Sunshine, sweet-smelling flowers, clean sheets, sober honest Georgian books in little recesses on the landings; it could have been before the war, you know; before the idea of war.'

'A pretty idyll,' Anne said drily. 'You must admit, though, it all sounds rather fortuitous and temporary. Was the sunshine home-made too, or did winter still come, in this warless world? And I presume the garden had to be dug?'

He kept back the biting reply to her sourness. 'Yes. There was a gardener. I was there only once; I can't imagine it in winter.'

'What made them so happy, anyway, what were they like?' she persisted. 'As boring as the Farmers?'

He still tried to contain his anger but despite the objective tone it overflowed. 'They wouldn't have understood what you said just then. At least—on hearing it they would have looked a little puzzled, and afterwards they would have said to each other: "I wonder what it is she wants?" '

He had hurt her, he knew that. From the quiet way she gave up fighting he knew he had hurt her. Unnecessarily she rearranged the remaining dishes, her head bent. 'Why don't you go to bed, Paul?' she suggested, busily scraping. 'I can manage these.'

'No, let me help. In fact' (but it came too late) 'let me do them for you. You're tired.'

'You're awfully charitable all of a sudden,' she said, with her face still hidden from him. 'What sin have you committed now?'

'No sin,' he said. 'No sin but loving you too much.'

She laughed. 'Not true, but never mind. Please go to bed, Paul, really; I won't be long.'

Being nice, for short periods, was not so very difficult. He felt an access of tenderness for her. 'Was the party ghastly for you, darling? Let's give another, then, for the people you like—all the unhappy, evil, interesting ones.'

'Oh, I don't like them,' she said seriously. 'They fascinate me, that's all. I wish I liked good people. Sometimes I try to remember if I like anyone . . .'

12

'And do you?' he asked.

'I can think only of you.' She turned fully towards him. He said quickly, 'I'll wait for you, then, upstairs.'

'And Roderick,' she added. 'I like him, good, or happy, or not.'

Anne

I saw a man pursuing the horizon;
Round and round they sped.
I was disturbed at this;
I accosted the man.
'It is futile,' I said,
'You can never . . .'
'You lie,' he cried,
And ran on.

Stephen Crane

1

What would give me happiness?

The question assumes much : that happiness can be attained; and it implies more : for instance, that to attain happiness is desirable. Most people do, I think, accept these things.

I do not.

In childhood it was different; that question occupied me strangely, in childhood : 'What would give me happiness?'

There was a park where I used to walk, in my childhood. An adult must have accompanied me always, yet in recollection I always seem to be alone; and though I must have walked in that park in every season of the year, to my memory the time is always autumn, the day always clouded still, and a little sombre, after rain. My feet push aside, thoughtfully, the wet leaves : the leaves of sycamore, I remember, green, but already speckled with brown; ash, in bunches that crackle despite their moisture; plane, for the district was suburban; other leaves, whose names I knew once, and now do not recall.

The ritual never varied; already, both pleased and mournful,

I knew where I—where we—had to go. We—I—passed the first long narrow lake and on the bridge over the next I stopped, as I always stopped, yet for barely a moment, to see if the golden pheasant was visible today. Because of his name, his colour, though rusty, for me was always gold.

Then footsteps thudded and rebounded over the sodden, hunched little bridge; surreptitiously I fingered its trellis-work, which was made from live branches: rough-hewn, blackish, thorny, truculent. And suddenly (more suddenly now, perhaps, than then) I was at the well.

Inevitably it was called the wishing-well. To wish was the sole purpose of my visit, or the only purpose I owned to myself, then. For now, it appears to me that this was the least of my reasons. Firstly, the well itself had a fascination. It was not pretty—the reverse. The water was stagnant and gloomy, choked with dank, listless leaves. It was not really a proper well but a pool, guarded in front and to one side by a short stony wall, and above by a little pointed roof. At another side its water, had movement been possible, would have merged into that of the lake. But it was set back, that was one attraction: set back so far that it could easily be passed even by those who knew where it stood. Also, it was malevolent. Any wish it granted must surely go awry; but then it never did grant one's wishes, and I had no confidence that it would. I always expected a frog, or sullen toad, to emerge from it and sit there moving the muscles of its enigmatical throat; or a bell, harsh and ominous, startlingly to ring out; or an old woman to appear menacingly behind me, demand my business, and refuse to let me go. None ever did.

'Go on then, make your wish!' the impatient voice would say.

Yes, there must always have been a grown-up with me.

Reluctantly, I picked up a stone. I should have liked more time to choose; this was not weighty enough, neither jagged, nor sufficiently smooth, not pleasant to the touch. Postponing the moment as long as possible, I drew back my right arm; aimed; and threw. The twinkling luminiferous ripples dispersed before I had time to appreciate them, always, and I was desolate, wanting to be immediately home again in front of the fire.

'Did you wish?'

Hastily I wished, and nodded.

'How is it you always get those black smudges on your fingers?'

I was asked many unanswerable questions in my childhood, but no one ever asked what I wished. Invariably it was that the person I loved would fall in love with me. I was in love often, perhaps always—but secretly, for I disliked derision, and few adults take seriously the romances of any child.

Would happiness have been to have my love returned?

Happiness would have been to do what then I never dared: to drop into the waters not a stone, but a penny. To throw money into wells, even wishing-wells, and once in a lifetime, would have been accounted by my family an extravagance: not, that is, materially, but an extravagance of the spirit. Years later, when, as a secretive, now orphaned, sixteen-year-old, I used to go alone into the park to smoke and to brood, once I threw into the wishing-well not a stone, nor a penny, but a half-crown: my last half-crown. I should have liked it to be a golden sovereign.

My idea of happiness had often altered. Once it was embodied in a story-book someone had given me: *The Magic Walking-stick*. First, I remember, the stick had to be twirled, then there must have been a rune to cast, a charm to mutter —but finally whoever possessed the talisman would be conveyed, in a trice, wherever he wished to go. So far as I recall there was no land, at that time, which I especially desired to see, yet for days, for weeks, for months, a whole enchanted year or more of childhood, chancing upon such a walking-stick was my secret vision of happiness, and I longed for it passionately.

Happiness now seems to me something like one of those vast, elegant stoppered bottles of lovely shape and glowing colour—deep emerald, ruby red—still seen sometimes high on a dusty shelf in the shop of an old-fashioned pharmacist. I used to wonder what such forgotten jars or limbecs might contain, and to dream, when I was a child, of possessing one. The dream did not fade, it was relinquished, slowly, with regret. Only amid the mingling delicious *pot-pourri* of a herbalist's shop : cool fragrances of lavender, peppermint, husky jessamine; cloves, with their sharper spice; rich sandalwood, stealthy mordancies of orange-water or of bergamot would my slender-necked, my sweetly curving phial have been at home; and even the herbalist could never possess it. So it is with happiness; light, colour, beauty of form can never be owned or captured.

The wonderful garden, just round the corner, was not happiness. The wonderful garden was peace. Happiness, at that time, meant pleasure, not good, and peace meant contentment, not pleasure. Yet whether the garden would still be peace tomorrow, or what it had been yesterday, I did not know. Of the wonderful garden I was a little afraid; certainly in summer, when a communicable reason for visiting it, its abundance of flowers, had arrived. And autumn was for the wishing-well, and in winter, when I asked to walk there, I was told it was 'miserable'. Lonely it was, I could see, and silent, but I never agreed that it was miserable, for if I had chosen I could have made it brilliant with flowers, and I liked its benches best when they were sad, damp, unpeopled. The wonderful garden in the park was under a spell.

It was green, and it was silent. It was solitary. I was a solitary child. I think I should have turned into someone of greater worth if I had never come into contact with another living person. On an island of rocks smashed by the storming sea, I would have discovered sooner that my purpose was to paint, and the different sorts of promiscuity I sampled, so many substitutes for death, would have remained untasted. It would have been better for me, better by far, to snatch up whatever came to hand—bone, like the Bushmen; stone; a stub of treasured pencil; a pointed reed such as Van Gogh used at Arles—and cut, hack, scrawl out or gouge the necessary, urgent records of relationships created by gale and spray and lightning-flash, than patiently, in a yawning hygienic studio, to suffer the bland eye of a man who could correct my line because he had never heard thunder smite or watched the sea engulf the sand.

Other gardens must have blended, through memory's soft betrayals, with the garden I knew in my childhood. But though their thorns attract me like the twisted gorse Graham

Sutherland discovered on the cliff, blackened, burnt, savage, it contains no sempiternal roses. None of my beloved cherry trees shower there their snow, nor does my garden resemble the orchards in which, when the world stopped writhing, Vincent the Dutchman saw the trunks blue, blue as the delicate bright sky that sang against tumults (pink, white) of exploding blossom. My garden is stark. My garden is bleak. My garden is filled with winter's desolation and its solitude. I do not see it in any way as a recollection whose source lies eastward in Eden; it is too clear for that. It is silence backing before the tread of an intruder's steps; loneliness none the less lonely for my lonely presence; a clarity of green ground and black implacable trees. It is not heaven; heaven repels me. It is not happiness; happiness I reject. It is only the image I have one day to set down on canvas: the last picture I shall paint.

*

Painters should not think too much, lest in the sun they dazzle. I shift my head, and pools of light, seas of colour, lakes of shadow, shift with me; I swim through them like a fish, expert, if gaping. I hardly think I shall ever be able to give my loaves, or my bottles of wine, the eternal stillness Chardin searched out for his, but I should be pleased beyond all measure if I attained one day to that lesser grace: of rendering in paint, with absolute fidelity, a single arrested moment of passion, whether it be rage, or pain, or the most inexplicable love, so that through the portrait I might come at last to my garden.

*

Celia could sit for the portrait of a saint: for a St Joan, especially. It is strange, in a way, that I have never yet painted her; or is it so strange? The short honey-gold hair and the brown eyes alone are not Celia, nor the look as if she might suddenly snatch out a sword and tell you to follow, confident that you would go. There is something she has lost that was essential; the sweetness no longer holds the same power, or potency, and to find out why would wreck a world.

*

Everyone grows older. That is not it. It is not years alone that separate her from the slender girl in the candy-striped blouse, whose skirt swung with such lightness and vigour from her hips on the sunlit mornings when she passed below my window. A hundred other students took the same path, but it was always she whom I watched. I can see, too clearly, that tremendously determined, yet so delicate, so resilient walk, and the welcoming smile of such irresistible radiance for anyone who entered her room. Two years younger than I, what she has lost is not mere youth, of that I am certain.

*

Although her father—Stephen, the first, the most hopeless, of my many hopeless loves—acted as my guardian (even, informally, till just before his death, a few years after I had come of age), she and I met but rarely during the vacations. At home the dominant personality was that of her mother, a brusque, brisk, business-like feminist who, having produced a litter or two of children under the impression that they were easier to rear than horses, was still somewhat surprised that, of a lusty brood, Celia and Roderick, the fragile and the incomprehensible, should be the ones to survive. Whether all three of us fled her—she was redoubtable—or whether it was each other's society that we shunned would be difficult now to determine; at all events I reached my eighteenth birthday without realizing that Celia meant to become a missionary, and she must have hesitated still longer to include me among the objects of her mission.

*

Perhaps, on the whole, Roddy was the chief cause of my own habitual flight. He was wild, a truer *fauve* than I. We never spoke; we were too shy to speak; shyness and speechlessness

22

made our encounters totally unnerving. Our taste in hiding-places was unfortunately so similar that the effort to escape each other resembled trying to play chess with oneself and lose. In the end a system silently developed whereby when he was at the piano I might go where I liked, no questions asked, and at other times, I remaining in the music room, the choice was his. The code of behaviour this enshrined was the most useful thing I learned from any of the Farmers, though I was also taught, by Stephen, Lithuanian, and how to play the classical guitar. There may have been some debts, too, to his wife, now so long dead, who coped with most problems then by issuing an imperturbable command to 'Leave it on the table', for it was certainly upon a table that I left ('lost' would hardly be the word) my virginity.

*

When, at about the same time, I became aware of my attrac-tion to Celia, I feared it might contain a Lesbian element, but its strangeness had causes more disturbing still. I did not want to plunge head first into religion, dive through the waters that terrified me, and come up to find no deity, but Celia alone. Whenever she asked me over for coffee I suspected a catch, and waited in dreadful embarrassment while she looked out a record, or casually offered me fondants innocuous, home-made. At last, despairingly, and completely devoid of faith, I would start off about God myself. She replied to my remarks without leading the discussion onwards; no advice came from her; I went away puzzled and confused.

Though her repose is still there the serenity has gone. No longer does one expect her to leave suddenly for the wilder-ness, armed only with a shining faith. I am not even sure she still believes, and to doubt it is appalling. If for the moth the hot flame is heaven, then better for it to singe its wings there than fly helplessly round and never stop. Yet I hardly feel, if her faith remains no longer, that it was lost; surrendered, I should rather say—but for what?

*

Yes, Celia must be painted, but first I need to do some more self-portraits. Narcissism, many would immediately declare. It is hard to decide whether they most lack charity, intelligence, humility or candour. Certainly they can never have looked through his own disenchanted eyes at Rembrandt, or noticed the merciless absorbed veracity of Cézanne. For the painter, 'my own face' means the useful measure, always with him, of the progress of a skill. 'Occupation', says my passport, 'student.'

Sitters, besides, grow moody when no painting is being done. Yet the first thing I need to establish is not the subject's character, but an awareness of the human presence impinging on its ground; shape, next, with its dimensions; only afterwards, the disposition of the details, and their colour and intensity and the light. If you stare at a man long enough, thinking of him as sheer form, he begins to wonder who he is. So I go back most frequently to Anne Rivers, student, her haunted face, her black streaming hair.

I am so many people. This is true of everybody, but most obvious in oneself, since though there may be, for instance, a thousand characters in Paul, there are only a few that he will show to each other person. Only at a party can revelations about familiar people occur. There, different masks are worn. There, mankind may suddenly turn to a race of robots, or a lover be seen through the eyes of someone else—as when, this evening, I saw Paul as if I were Celia, and discovered what it was like to be silently in love with him.

If it is not possible to hate and to like simultaneously, I wonder what I feel for Celia. Did Paul realise, when we spoke of St Joan, that I was really talking about her? Yet I admire Celia; I love her; and for the untutored peasant girl who would rather be burned than give up her delusions the proper feeling is awe.

*

I have been what the world calls 'mad', so when I apply the word to others I intend by it no insult. Paul says it would help if I tried to think of the dark and swarming periods as a curable illness of the mind; but living for several years a yard from the brink has reduced the importance of nomenclature.

24

Best would be to concentrate upon my paintings: so many inches of canvas; the paint to cover it with; the struggle to be free of an idea that itself struggles to come out—as the embryo struggled to come out of my womb, but I will not think of the embryo, Paul says it would not help. I will think of the canvas, the pictures, the paint.

*

I use the wrong medium, people who know things about art tell me when they watch me on the job, and to anyone who thinks the point of oil paints is the mixing of oil with them it must seem horribly true. Lovely luminous linseed! I never use it.

I squeeze the tube and the rich paint gleams like toothpaste, it squirms out glistening—as the embryo came out from my womb, but I will not think of the embryo. I will fight the paint with the brush and my fingers and thumbs and the knife, till the work is finished, all the ugliness has been purged away, and what is left on the canvas has no connexion with me at all.

But finishing one's work is terrible, because then it goes into a gallery and people want varnish put on it and the critics come and look, and talk about its moulding. Moulding! What a word to use to the tiger still dripping blood from someone else's meat! While my fight is on, there is just such a gory mess as that. If a man did it there would be talk of mauling, but when a woman makes a relief painting she must have moulded it. We were given votes only to prevent us from asking for anything more dangerous, like freedom of speech, action and thought.

Men, except for obstetricians, do not have to see the embryo or the foetus squirm from the womb, glistening, attached to the end of an intricately twisted, disposable string. In spite of that, going into a field black with crows, Van Gogh shot himself. 'Misery will never end.'

Misery never ended, despite brother Theo, his loans and ministrations. Misery never ends, though at least I only had to speak with Roderick once this evening, and then not alone. Misery, for us, will never end till Janice die.

2

It was eight years ago, and involved a different Anne Rivers:
tougher, still more stubborn, with a blaze of energy I now
wonder at. Odd as the details of the programme may have
been, it was packed; I expected to complete twelve hours of
work a day: not the occasional meal or time off with coffee
and cigarettes to think, but twelve hours' onslaught on the
canvas; twelve hours of struggling with the idea in my head.

People had warned me to let up. The advice was good, so I
ignored it. Soon I was slap in the middle of what I described,
calmly enough, as a 'fallow period', thus implying it began and
it would end, it was going to benefit the cultivation and I had
exercised some choice about it. What it seemed like, though,
was complete sterility: sterility before and after time,
sterility infinite. Nothing I did was any good, neither painting,
talking, nor making love. If I went to take up a brush, the
contemplated subject turned to mirage, and there was desert
all round me again. It felt like death.

In the middle of it all Alan went away because I refused

to marry him. When, after about five days, I began to sober up once more, someone called Flicky seemed to be living in the flat. Apart from being a kleptomaniac, she never made her bed. She told me we had met in a pub and I had fallen for her hard-luck story. It seemed likely enough.

One day I opened a fortnight's mail, from which I gathered that there was a big exhibition that included some of my early work. I told Flicky that I was going out, so if she intended staying another night she must make her bed herself and light the gas under a pie I had just prepared. She went into an Irish huff and said she did not wish to spend even *two* more nights anywhere she was not welcome but she would willingly make her bed all the same. I stopped myself from pleading with her to stay by remembering that the bed we were both calling hers belonged in fact to me; but that raised the question of why, then, I did not want to make it, and I was in no condition to deal with moral problems. Intense relationships with women easily reduce me to tears even when I am completely sober. In the end I gave her most of my loose change to save her the trouble of looking for it, and told her that on the Embankment there were no beds to make. Right, she said, if that was what I wanted she would go there. I excused her from awaiting my return.

*

Though it was interesting to discover how good some of the earliest pictures were, the main surprise was to see the problems I could now solve and had not been able to before. But its blood was red, it all had passion, and I shied away from thinking I might never reach such heat again. The picture I had made of Kiri just before he threw me over suddenly confronted me: that love and hate glaring back at me as in the old days, brown flesh and a black heart put down with such anger and remorseless accuracy by a brush I had held. The savage black outlines around the scarlet robe had been an afterthought; but what a good one! Like the leaded transoms and mullions of church windows, the ebony which at first seemed to break up the design was seen ultimately to hold together its various parts. Those brilliant reds and golds

27

would otherwise, clashing together, have raged without control, and taken away the attention meant for Kiri's massive snarling head. Perspective had necessarily been sacrificed; the juxtaposition of the black and red had a flattening effect, eliding the third dimension; but the stylised grandeur that ensued, the heraldic splendour of barbarous pain, was worth that or any other price.

*

Yet there was so much of Kiri I had failed to convey. I had no feeling for him left; between us he and I had killed it. The pity was that though he had shaped my definition of love for all time, love—*my* love—was lacking from this canvas. At the time of painting I had not shaken him off, the vast idea of him. When I had learned to show his callousness unflinchingly, not portraying it with resentment or shame, but accepting it without any reserve, I might become a painter. Formally the thing was all right—curiously, since here I had left form to take care of itself. The composition could not be faulted, and I had neither idealised nor caricatured. The passion came at the wrong angle, that was all—all, and essential. For if I could not paint with love my Christ who murdered me, how could I hope to paint a universal god, and accept my share in murdering him?

A low, clear, golden voice was speaking, diagonally across the room from me. I caught my own name, and involuntarily listened.

'You know her, then?'

'We haven't met for ages, but she's a great friend of Celia's. Steve was her guardian, as a matter of fact!'

He had said it with studied nonchalance, but imparted an unmistakable air of enjoying reflected glory. I felt both flattered and a little disappointed, annoyed.

To go over to them at once was impossible; I turned back to the other room, where a MacBryde had caught my attention when I came in. Nodding to the somnolent guard there, I recouped my losses on Flicky by taking a handful of florins from one of the bowls before ruffling through the sumptuous catalogue. It was prefaced by a quotation from Matisse:

28

'Expression for me is not to be found in the passion which blazes from a face or which is made evident by some violent gesture. It is in the whole disposition of my picture—the place occupied by the figures, the empty space around them, the proportions—everything plays its part.'

That, I thought ruefully, is it. For all the play of the spotlight, the background to my portrait of Kiri is completely inert.

I went through into the main room again and moved straight over the man and girl, who were looking at my *Memories of Hell*.

'... rather a bad reputation.'

'Hallo,' I said. 'It's Roddy, isn't it?'

He turned. I had forgotten his extraordinary likeness to the Charioteer of Delphi : thick lips, solid jaw, long lovely curve of brow continued into the nose; rather staring eyes; short crisp hair. He put out his hand just as the Charioteer holds the reins—high—and I fumbled in taking it.

'Good Lord! We were just ... talking about you.' He turned back, slightly confused, to his companion, a soft, flushed, wispy girl.

'Is it true,' she asked, 'you don't use any binding agent?' She had been reading the sumptuous catalogue.

'By binding agent,' I said gently, 'they mean oil. No, I don't use any oil, yet.'

'Then, the pictures will ...?'

'Not actually fall to pieces, but probably crack after a year or so.' I looked at Roddy. 'It was I who had the bad reputation?'

He coloured, but she was irrepressible. 'Do you think it's quite moral to sell them, if they're not going to last?'

'I think it's damned immoral to buy them,' I retorted. 'The only time I ever tried to tell people that the pictures, being done for my own benefit, might flake, we had bloody queues all over the pavements waiting to learn the prices, and the critics insinuated it was remarkable to what lengths I'd go to get publicity.'

'The pictures are done just for yourself? But you sell them, don't you?' she said.

'They're experiments.' My eyes met Roddy's again. 'The

29

equivalent of scales.' He nodded. 'But if people want to buy them, I don't complain, because after all I have to make a living.'

'But you think they're fools, the purchasers?'

'Yes,' I replied, 'I think they're greedy fools.'

'I don't understand you.'

By this time Roddy and I understood each other very well.

'They could come and look; there's no need to possess. Eventually, though—they should wait . . . I might do a picture worth the possessing, one day.' I scanned the gallery, and jerked my head at the portrait of Kiri. 'Nearly there with that one.'

'Another enemy!' I remarked cheerfully on her departure to lunch with her mother.

'She's an unscrupulous little beast,' said Roddy. The observation might have been meant for a warning. It was hard to tell. At any rate he had not given it the tone of a moral judgement.

He took my arm, and stated, with more forcefulness than I had somehow expected, '*You're* going to lunch with me.'

'Indeed I'm not; I'm carrying you off to my flat, where you'll be fed nectar and ambrosia and a huge helping of apple pie.'

The speculation of his regard was manifest.

I inquired, 'You suspect me of an urge to seduce you?'

'If you felt such an urge, I think I should rather like it.'

'I do feel it,' I found myself crazily saying.

When we reached the flat I was still thinking: 'But he's a *boy*, I must be five years older!'

'Flicky!' I called. She was gone. I started towards the kitchen; Roddy, who had already opened another door, caught me by the shoulders. His hands slid down. Unsteadily I pulled the bedroom door shut behind us, closed my eyes, and, my right hand on the nape of my neck, sought, with my left, the zip of the dress. Women, whether from modesty, patience, hypocrisy or a sense of the dramatic, retain till last their most essential garment, surrendering it with an air of unwillingness delicious to the beholder; not so men.

'You might,' I suggested, eyes still closed, 'take off your

30

shirt too. Psychologically, it would leave me at less of a disadvantage.'

*

Gold was pouring all over my face. Through the lids it beat, trembled, vibrated. My lashes quivered; my eyes flickered open, shut again under the dazzle of sun and a darkness equally brilliant. I opened them wide at last, and almost yelled when the silhouette took shape as the Charioteer of Delphi, burnished with sunlight, staring down at me.

'Have you done that many times?' he asked.

'What? Slept with a man I'd not met since he was sixteen?'

The reference to his age annoyed him, just as questions about biography annoy me. There is no connexion between what I did yesterday and what I might do tomorrow.

I said, coolly, 'I'm usually a little more temperate about my affairs, as a matter of fact.' And thought, immediately, of Kiri. The explanation of why my recent painting had lacked fire had just occurred to me : I had burned myself out on Kiri.

Pleased with that conclusion—fires can be refuelled—I snuggled back under the sheets, forgetting about my nineteen-year-old Charioteer. He uncovered me again, and again I felt a rush of desire. I pushed him gently back. 'Lie down.'

'But I want you.'

I deepened to my bedroom voice. 'Lie down.'

*

He was astonished. 'I didn't think ...'

'Didn't think what?' I murmured through a mouthful of pillow, rolled over on to my back again and stretched bliss-fully from my toes to the tips of my long long fingers, laughing and exhausted.

'Well—that nice women did things like that.' He looked down at me suspiciously, waiting to be furious if I mocked.

'Nor did Lucretius, but at least he lived a few centuries earlier than you. You think nice women seduce their friends'

31

brothers? You are *sweet*—no one's called me a nice woman for years.'

He was sullen.

I slid to the edge of the bed and hung over it, searching for my sandals, then dropped a kiss on his antagonised back, took a shower, put on a dressing-gown and went to see about food.

He followed me. When playing cook I cannot stand having men near by. They wear such a pathetic hangdog expression. Patiently I led him into the dining-room, indicated bottles, pulled out a chair and thrust some Oriental erotica into his hands. Then I went back into the kitchen, threw together a salad and fried some aubergines with tomato, onion, potatoes and mushrooms while the steak sizzled luscious under the grill. Flicky had faithfully obeyed my instructions about the oven. We must have just missed each other. Feelings of guilt dissipated when I noticed she had removed the kitchen bottle of rye. And suddenly I was terribly hurt that she had left me. It's only when they leave you that you know whom you love.

A swig at the cooking-sherry, which dispersed the slight fog on my tongue, reminded me that somewhere there ought to be a bottle of Oloroso.

'Roddy!' I called. 'Is there any sherry out, or only gin?'

'Gin!' he yelled back.

'Look in the cupboard. If there's any claret, we could have that too.'

Despite strong coffee, in the bathroom afterwards we both became truculent. 'Don't imagine,' I told him, 'that because you slept in my bed this afternoon you'll automatically be sleeping there tonight.'

But there was another bottle of claret in the sideboard, and plenty of gin on top. When I awoke next morning under the Delphic Charioteer it occurred to me for the first time how lucky it might after all be that Alan had gone away. Since I have difficulty in keeping up with the pace of events, I burst into tears, and had to be comforted.

And then, oh! it was spring, and I in love again, hopelessly as ever before, bluebell skies and buds of blossom, young rain, the amorous smell of grass. Six sweet months passed,

I wept into the empty bed, wanting to be married with him, bestraddled by him, for ever and ever.

*

Roddy was to expect me by the first afternoon train. Having, however, woken early after rather a bad night, I climbed the malodorous staircase at eleven, relieved to be at the end of a journey that had been full of fog and dirt, and to have found so far no cause for the sense of foreboding that had pervaded the travelling air.

The sound of laughter came from his room. I halted, wondering if I ought to have telephoned from the station.

' . . . but not this afternoon, someone's coming to see me after lunch,' said the golden voice.

' . . . ?'

'Oh, not really. Anne Rivers, the painter . . . friend of my mother's, though, so I can't . . . other time, instead?'

The greater guilt belongs to the betrayed. On reaching London I dispatched a telegram : *Best not to come stop no explanations Rivers*. I had forgotten with what ruthlessness former affections can be amputated during the first term, and what unthinkable lapses of time separate the nineteen-year-old from those who are his senior by some five or six or seven years.

An aching heart is much like an aching tooth; one is angry with oneself for possessing it, but if its removal must be postponed, alcohol, or deceptive drugs, may sufficiently dull the pain. Perhaps, one vaguely thinks, it may forget to return.

Profligate, reeling into trains and out again disapproved of, I debouched, debauched, at the Strand, wove my way towards the National Gallery, and brooded, brandy-filled, before the Pisanello *Vision of St Eustace*. No other painter could without blasphemy depict the Crucifixion and pay it so little heed. One stands and admires the young fairy-tale knight on his fairy-tale charger; pores, curious with brandy, over the arched, intent and leaping hound tracking the heels of a rabbit discreetly anxious to escape; watches, bemusedly, luminous visionary birds that rocket like lightning across the heavens;

or hunts, with the rider, the stag whose turning grace is as legendary and remote as a unicorn's.

Back home I lurched, now savage on rum, into the smell of paint, a frenzy of work, reds bloody as rare steak and the thick juicy pleasure of laying them on, before slumping prostrate upon my virginally aching bed, the fumes of nausea, a vacant night.

For there was a complication, to be dealt with in the morning.

*

Dr Wlenkowicsz was away, his unctuous secretary informed me. When would he return? Mmm, Dr Wlenkowicsz *maight* be returning, mmm, at the end of a fortnaight. When *would* he return? 'N a fortnoigh', madam. Madam was wishin' to mike an appintmen'? She coughed.

'. . . Anne Rivers. Yes, Anne Ribble. No, Ann with*out* an "e".'

Sixteen days later I was sitting on the edge of a chair, watching his pudgy hands, myself watched by a pudgier male nurse.

'You can't,' Wlenkowicsz said thoughtfully, 'marry the man?'

'No.'

He doodled on the blotting-paper.

'He's married,' I said, and, by dint of holding my breath, turned scarlet.

'Ah? With children?'

'Yes.'

'Sad.'

'Yes.'

The examination finished, I returned to the chair before the desk.

'At such an advanced stage,' he suavely bargained, 'it might be necessary for you to go into my private nursing home. . . .'

'How much?' I asked.

Ann Ribble, shorthand typist, carelessly clad, might be able to afford one hundred pounds, for her carelessness.

'If everything went well,' he said with a small smile, 'a hundred pounds.'

'I couldn't find an amount like that.'

We looked, with distaste, into each other's eyes.

'A second opinion?' he suggested.

'For no second opinion and no nursing home, how much?'

'The second opinion is necessary under the present law. But with no nursing home—there is a risk, you understand.' He looked at my eyes again. 'Seventy pounds,' he said abruptly.

'When shall I come?'

He consulted a diary. 'Next Tuesday? At ten in the morning?'

I slid swiftly into my coat, clutching it to me away from his hands.

'For breakfast only a cup of tea,' said the male nurse conspiratorially. 'Bring two sanitary towels.'

At the door Wlenkowicsz stopped me. 'Not a cheque, if you please.'

And if I die, not on your premises, I thought.

*

By twelve o'clock on Tuesday, the child inside me was struggling to commit suicide, frantically wriggling and squirming inside my belly. The sensation was one I seemed to have experienced before, but I could not recall when, or think what it was. Antiseptic splashings of hands and clankings of bowls were taking place behind me; I turned, and the male nurse, coming over, gently shook his head, looked at me sympathetically, and moved back out of sight.

The tugging became more slithery, more desperate. At that I remembered: I had felt it when holding a fish that fought to get free from the hook. Suddenly I felt horribly faint, and my mind was going blindly round and round, gaping, like a goldfish in its bowl; I started to tremble violently, and Wlenkowicsz, smiling, his face fat with the price of tax-free slaughter, laid one of his pudgy hands on my thigh and said. 'You're not frightened, are you?' He patted me.

I closed my eyes and opened them again, and my head became clearer. 'No,' I said. I even smiled.

Not frightened. Sick.

3

Jasmine's 'Exclusive Interview with Anne Rivers', headlined 'THOSE GREEDY FOOLS THE PUBLIC', appeared that month, the day before the opening of my new exhibition. I arranged for all the main papers to be delivered, disconnected the telephone, and went to bed preserved in alcohol.

At the opening, reporters trailed me round and round the galleries.

'Have you any comments on Miss Donald's article, Miss Rivers, please?'

'Jasmine,' I said briefly, 'is an old friend.'

'Of,' I muttered into my whisky, 'Old Nick at least.'

Awaiting what the weeklies would say about the new pictures was more than usually nightmarish. The general response turned out to be one less of fury than of the polite incomprehension that can doom a whole career. Already acutely depressed, I was utterly despondent by the time I reached the last, and most influential, of the week's reviews, which was signed—to make it, I thought with suicidal calm, the more effectively damning—not by their regular critic, who appeared to dislike all paintings and their makers equally, but by one Paul Hawkes, a name I seemed to recollect having heard Roddy mention : perhaps one of his Wykehamist friends.

This lengthy notice was in fact decisive. To have commented only upon the current exhibition of Anne Rivers' work, he wrote, would have been to do scant justice to a talent whose outstanding feature had always been the richness of its variety. He proposed, so far as his limits would allow, to trace her wandering but purposeful progress from the first distant foothills (I pulled a face) to the minor peak where— gathering her strength to essay the ultimate pinnacle—she was now encamped. Donne's second *Satyre* might, he thought, be relevant here. . . .

The accumulated effects of several days' potations were making themselves felt. I had a coffee and two cigarettes, and thought about going abroad; then recalled that, now I needed it, I no longer possessed the fare.

Returning pessimistically to the article, I suddenly saw that despite several attacks of review-writers' gut-rot, its author had an adequate understanding of both my craft and his own. Where something had gone wrong, he saw what, he saw why; and sometimes he was able even to suggest how an improvement might be made. To the first pictures of the series *Towards Redemption* he offered only praise. 'These studies of a black Christ', he said, '—most notably *Burn Him for a Witch* —have a depth of morality new to her own work, and novel in this decade. She has painted her *J'accuse*, and a world stands condemned; the intent and unshakable dispassion she manifests can make her an artist uncomfortable to meet. It can no longer be doubted that she is a major European painter, engaged, at close quarters, with major, and formidable, tasks.'

The major European painter, giggling irresponsibly, still had the evening papers to deal with, but Jasmine Donald had deemed it prudent to hold her fire, and their mood was benign. A telegram reached me next day, informing me that an application filed for a travelling-scholarship (and by me already forgotten) had been successful : I could now choose where I should least dislike to be alive.

37

Spain, I thought at first, because of Valázquez. How his failure to see the point of his own creations can haunt one!—that ominous figure poised in the doorway in *Las Meninas*, which he treats as casually as if it were only the apex to one of the composition's many triangles! Yet once that figure has been noticed, the true focal point is lost; no longer is any attention paid to the vicious little Infanta central in the foreground, going off into a royal sulk, petulant, bored by dog and dwarf, head averted from her maid. Then triangles previously unseen reveal themselves: self-portrayed painter, maid, dog; maid, dwarf, dog; Infanta, other maid, dog—till the brain reels, textures, facial expressions, disappear, and all that remains is the aloof figure eternally watching from the doorway. And by Velázquez not Picasso only has been haunted, but Francis Bacon, the latter by a painting whose original he is alleged never to have seen: the portrait of Innocent X, splendid and unholy under shimmering vestments in a richly ornamented chair. Having looked at the cunning pontifical face, the El Greco lightning-play of silks and satins, the papal ring on the limp hand of that Velázquez portrait, whose, one wonders, in the Bacon interpretation is the terrifying shriek?

In Holland there would be the Van Goghs, and some of the Rouaults in France . . . but Holland and France have become the ghosts of my children, a pond of goldfish tugging at my barren womb.

I will travel, perhaps, to Méjico, to think about time, and gods, and barrenness, and death.

*

Mexico City was, first of all, the airport at dawn, where, while he swept the floor, an old young man sang the saddest song I have ever heard, ending in a perfectly cadenced question-mark that he knew had no answer. It was, later, the two volcanoes: Popocatépetl, the Smoking Mountain, and the white woman Ixtaccíhuatl, as for every tourist who has spent a day there. Afterwards it was death: death everywhere, tasted and savoured; the smell of flies cooked in sugar on sticky green figs under a torrid sun; vultures above the mountains unhurriedly gliding, black, sometimes quite motionless, till they should scent a corpse, and fall.

On the pavements, beggars crouched waiting to die. The first day, one put too much money into their outstretched shaking hands, rather than look; and the next day, less money, still not looking; and the third, overcome with fury that they should still be there, still about to die, none. An old man with a trailing tremulous voice talked about *limosna* (was it alms?), about *caridad*, and stretched out *por el amor de Dios, señorita linda*, another of those shaking hands. Quivering with the intensity of one's shame, one said '*Trabajo para ganar mi vida, yo*', staring into the distance till the shuffling of his steps had ceased to be heard. I, I work for my living, am not, like you, eighty years old; and have no faith in the God who makes you crawl to me telling lies about my prettiness and His love.

One escaped from the dying into the ruins and museums to look at the dead: at Xipe Totec, Our Lord the Flayed One, legs too long, arms lopped off, mouth opened in a soundless scream, eyes narrowed, with empty sockets, face polished as if shining with sweat; at Mictlantecuhtli, a skull with bared teeth, everyone's vilest nightmare; at Tlaloc the Rain God with the sad mastiff's face, the vacant mouth sagging. Squat, broad, dreadfully smooth and flat figurines made the nights sleepless. Mexico was overpowering.

I retreated, fighting a staunch rearguard action, at first only as far as Teotihuacán, Place of the Gods, whose happy fierce jaguars seemed comparatively innocuous. In the waters of Tepantitla, the dead chased butterflies and dabbled their hands in the waters of the mountain assigned to them, flowers instead of speech tumbling from their mouths. I brooded in the sun about some codices that showed a group of sensitive-faced warriors in tall pointed hats and cotton armour; for one sensitive-faced warrior was standing on the legs of his prostrate opponent while preparing, with a smile, to club him thoughtfully to death.

During my absence Mexico City had contrived some new diversions, I noticed as I crossed the plaza back to my hotel. Pausing in the lobby, 'Why,' I asked, 'the chocolate skulls?'

Tomorrow was a big fiesta. Tomorrow was the Día de los Muertos: the Day of the Dead, or All Saints' Day. In the

39

plaza, effigies of Judas Iscariot would be burned. It would be very jolly, or was he perhaps saying holy? There would be fireworks, and feasting in the cemeteries. Okay?

With a shudder I thought about all the possibilities Hallowe'en in Mexico might hold.

Affably, there would be 'special meals', the manager added, 'very distinctive'.

I unconditionally surrendered.

At the airport the same saddest song was still being sung. I inquired if there was any empty seat on any aeroplane—preferably a jet. An hour or so later we landed at La Aurora. The question 'What country am I in?' invites a silly answer everywhere, so I mounted the steps of the post office and sent off some mail. It was Guatemala, in four languages the 'Land of Eternal Spring'.

4

The whole country is saturated in light, brimming with a meaningless happiness. Grief, horror, turn to apathy in the sun, so that on the pavement the beggar squats apparently unmoved by his own suffering, and the drunkard sleeps quietly, sprawled in front of someone else's house.

I knew as soon as I arrived that in Guatemala I would not be able to paint. It is a land full of pictures made trivial by the sun; the painting must be done later, from exile, not while such purity of light is still being absorbed into the skin. Her continued residence in the land of her birth may be what makes La Locha's brothel renowned through the whole sub-continent and beyond, for all the other celebrities pursue their work abroad. In Guatemala itself the only sensible plan is to begin nothing; then, there is no disappointment. Those who commence a work of art under that crystalline sky, regarding those blue mountains and their phantasmagoria of cloud, begin to say 'Tomorrow', and end as lazars. It can be seen in the first few minutes, from the way the Indian women, who are fond of their children, carry them slung on the hip, 'hekmek', as who should say, hotchpotch, or what-the-hell. Perhaps, too, it is why, when I remembered that this was the place where Celia had established, at long last, her mission, I made no attempt to find it or to let her know of my arrival; and why, as a result, she had departed before we met again.

I was also tired, and Guatemala is a good locale for rest.

*

So clean the streets are, after Mexico, so tranquil. There is dust, naturally, but the houses look as if early every morning they are washed down and carefully dried once more. Low, one-storeyed against earthquake, they are ice-cream colours, or the colours of fruits: lemon, orange, papaya, crushed strawberry, like the clouds above the mountains. And, like the clouds above the mountains, or the streets, which take, very softly, a rosy flush when, in the evenings, the light begins to fade, they are never exactly the same colour one hour as the next.

Unfortunately I am always in love with the last man, the last country, the finished painting, so the houses and the streets of Guatemala took on a melancholy air as the pining for Mexico grew. I wanted to hear again the saddest song. After Mexico everything Guatemalan seemed a trifle bland; above all, in Guatemala there was no *tequila*. *Tequila* is drunk with a lick of salt and a squirt of lemon; it smells like petrol; everyone who survives it attains immortality.

I stared at the walls of my room, which resembled turkish towelling, or, though two of them were green not pink, the pad with which rouge is applied. The first week I had kept furtively touching them, expecting them to have turned soft in the night. There was still no *tequila*, and besides, I was waiting for something to happen. Nothing ever did. I brooded. People began to ask if all the English were like me. Mine, I assured them, was a dying tribe.

Sometimes I went for a walk. In the streets there were very few dogs and no cats. It was noticeable how fast, in Guatemala, one's fingernails grew, and, to balance this, how seldom one's shoes wore out.

Still nothing happened. I looked at the map one day to make sure that Guatemala City was the capital of the Republic. There had been no mistake. The newspapers were full of vendettas, *crimes passionels*, kidnappings, vampirism and sheer unadulterated massacre. But apart from the occasional revolution it all took place off stage, elsewhere, behind one's back.

Then the insects began. First came the death-watch beetles, then the wood-lice, then the ants. One night I waited up till every ant climbing the flex of my lamp had been exterminated; then I lay down and saw them trekking in a long silent caravan across the ceiling. The bed pushed back, I went into the bathroom to fetch some water for splashing the clever little creatures down with, and a cockroach fell with a juicy plop into the basin, where, despite my kindly attempts to stab it, it perversely drowned. Obsessed first with the notion that some of the dog's fleas had reached my hair, I lowered myself balefully into bed at last, at last switched off the light—then jerked upright and put it back on in time to see a spider portentously hanging over the pillow. Next morning the streets were as tranquil and clean as ever. I entered the little public garden :

JARDIN DE M. PACHECOH

whose fountain and flowers had often attracted me as I passed.

'Are you a gringa?' an unpleasant little bullet-headed boy came from nowhere to demand.

I considered saying, 'Yes, if you're a dago', but instead replied, 'I'm from England.'

'The North Americans speak English too,' he said accusingly.

'Oh?' I observed.

His owlish elder brother made his way round from the other side of the fountain and shyly chimed in. 'You are of London?'

'Yes. Would either of you like to see my passport?'

The older boy flushed. He had only wanted to practise the Bouverie accent they taught him in school. The other one nodded, expectant.

I laughed suddenly. 'Don't go away,' I said to the shy boy.

'I had not the intention to molest you. It is so nice,' he replied laboriously. 'It is so nice in the sun.'

43

When we had agreed that nothing was more pleasant than the Guatemalan climate, mountains, hospitality, when I had complimented him on his command of American, and he had indignantly rescued me from a beggar of the more effusive sort, I moved to go. '*Adiós, pues.*'

'London must be nice too,' he said magnanimously, not believing it.

In the waters under the fountain there was a sudden flurry and flash.

He pointed. '*Cómo se llama en inglés?*'

'It's called a goldfish.'

'*Cómo?*'

'Goldfish,' I repeated. '*Dios.*'

'*Que le vaya bien, señorita. Que le vaya bien!*'

To suppose that the insects must decrease at the loftier altitudes was reasonable, and—unless they had already been planted on the top of Everest—it ought also to be possible to achieve a height at which there were no more Pepsi-Cola signs. We were already nearly five thousand feet up, but at the week-end I borrowed a horse and rode out of the city, away from the insects, away from the vendors of lottery tickets and *chicle*, into the cool blue mountains, alone at last with the goldfish swimming round my mind.

*

The winding track became steeper. Already the horse was tiring; I gathered the reins and tried to urge him forward, but it was no use; he jibbed. I dismounted. A great red Guatemalan moon, coloured from the smoke that must earlier have billowed up from scorched pine-branches, was sailing across a mass of cloud high in the sky. Silence was almost palpable. It would be good, but dangerous, to sleep here; I had no blanket, and on the mountains the nights can be cold. I stroked the horse's nose. He nuzzled against me for the sugar I had also forgotten, he blew into my hand and licked it, and I touched my lips a moment to his silky head. Then, jerking at the bridle, I began to walk; with a toss of the mane he followed me.

The soft brush brush of my riding-breeches, the slow dry

44

multiple clop of the horse's hooves, made mosaic rhythms in polychrome on the moonlit road. It was difficult to see ahead because of the ghostly children that blurred, rather than barred, the way.

There is always an alternative that could have been taken, always, always, always. That it was not taken never implies it did not exist. I *chose* the abortion; I chose it knowing it might mean barrenness; I *chose* barrenness: never to have his children, or mine with another man. Because—let us be realistic—one day another man there might be.

When I was a child, the other children at my first school used to play a game called 'Pinch-or-punch-or-join-in-the-ring'. They linked hands and ran about the playground stopping people; and sometimes they ran up to me and encircled me and chanted: 'Pinch-or-punch-or-join-in-the-ring?' The pinches were mean, and somehow shameful to receive; the punches could be very hard, especially if boys were playing. I will not pretend I had any scruple about hitting other children; if I refrained, it was probably because I preferred the more flexible weapon of words; but my aversion from joining in the ring was marked.

'Punch!' I replied, almost invariably.

'That child,' a teacher said of me once in my hearing, 'is antisocial.' I did not know what the word meant.

There was always a choice. It is shown by the fact that sometimes I condoned their vicious tweaks, occasionally I joined their ring, and once I stood in silence, surrounded by them, and refusing to play their game at all. In the end some pinched me, and some punched me, harder than usual, and as I still said nothing and would not cry to please them, they went away—laughing, or jeering, or (one or two) in thought. And, so as not to discuss what had happened, played a different game.

Therefore I must suppose that I could equally well have carried the child to term as had it killed; and that, if it once was born, I could then have throttled it myself or put it into a 'children's home', meaning an institution for those who have neither home nor childhood; or, somewhere, I could have made a warm place for it, and given it suck, and learned, touching it, to love in a different way.

And if I had taken the other role—if I had made the embryo my son or daughter—it would have been in the knowledge that I did it by choice and that I could as easily or with as much difficulty have played the assassin. The killer bends over the crib to soothe the baby's pains or loneliness or hunger, shakes a toy to make it smile, changes the small wet bundle, rocks it back to the serenity of sleep.

Therefore I must also suppose that when I committed what to the law is infanticide and murder to me, I had a motive. Today's acts are gratuitous, but for those of yesterday there is always a cause. And, having chosen hell, I must know what I suffer; must name the draught I have condemned myself to drink.

The flickering at the corners of my eyes increased. The sky suddenly contained streaks of silver. Thunder spoke. I stumbled, and, awakening again, looked around. In the long pause full of crinkles of lightning that followed, I tugged at the horse's head and raced, pulling him after me, through the trees. Then rain poured down in torrents, as fierce and violent as a shower turned on too far, soaking us to the skin. The horse reared, whinnying, as another bolt of thunder crashed and lightning immediately illumined the steaming foliage. I quietened him, mounted, kicked at his side, and we were off, stirrups swinging free, saddle, its girths too loose, wincing. The drumming of rain became so insistent that the man was beside me, yelling at the top of his voice, before I heard his mare approach. He caught at the reins and urged us with him over fallen logs, through thick squelching mud, slippery slithering leaves, up, and round a bend, then down, down, through more trees, and again down till we stopped before his *rancho*.

He gasped, and dashed the water from his hair. '*María, dónde está?*'

'*Ahorita voy, Carlitos, ahorita voy!*'

He turned to me. '*Pase adelante, señorita.*'

'*Gracias.*'

'*De nada,*' he answered.

'*Muchísimas gracias, señor,*' I repeated.

Maria entered. '*Ay, Dios!*' she exclaimed. She turned to him. '*Pobrecita!*'

'*Sí, pues,*' he said, laughing. 'You lost your way?' he asked me.

'I'm nearly always lost.'

Maria fetched water, blankets, a glass of warm *atol*. Carlitos waved it away. 'Brandy,' he said gruffly. She brought it. A hammock was slung for me.

'*Pase una buena noche, señorita,*' said Maria.

'*Igualmente. Buenas noches, Don Carlitos.*'

He bent his head. They went through into another room.

*

'You came from the city?' Maria asked at breakfast. Carlitos looked up.

'Yes,' I said, 'from the city. I shall not go back. Not to that city, nor to any other for a while.'

They nodded in complete understanding.

'Once,' said Carlitos, 'it was different.' He spread out his hands. 'Perhaps one day again. *Quién sabe?*'

'Who knows?' I agreed.

When he had gone, Maria came over to me and said firmly, 'There is room in this house. We would like you to stay as long as you wish.'

'Thank you, very much indeed. When I leave you will understand that it is because I am restless just now?'

'Of course.' She smiled. '*Quién sabe?* Perhaps you will come back.'

'*Sí. Tal vez, sí.*'

*

I stayed a long time, but one morning I told them that the next day I should depart; I wished to live alone for a while before returning to England, to paint.

'Ah, you're a painter, Ana?' said Carlitos. They had never asked.

'Yes, here it is not possible to paint,' he added. 'And you will be glad to be somewhere where there is no need to hang the Virgin on your wall, *verdad?*'

I smiled. Maria smiled too, for a different reason. She liked

47

me, but she had sensed that it was a little because of Carlitos that I was leaving, and she felt great relief that he would never know, even if it meant that my departure wounded him.

'There is an *hacienda* up there . . . ' He indicated the direction. 'I could take you, if you would wait until the end of the week.'

Maria said nothing.

'There's no need. I can find it, if you tell me the way.'

'Yes,' he responded thoughtfully. 'No one will hurt you, because you are not afraid.'

We said goodbye early that morning, and repeated that, who knows, I might come back, but two of us at least knew I never would.

5

Words, notes, or the strokes of a brush will blend, ambiguous, to such an extent that is hard to tell whether it is the greater gain or loss that their attributes cannot be isolated, and resist being fixed. 'Love', for instance, to me is a black rose, often rumoured, found by the very few: by Dido Queen of Carthage, yet not by Priam's son; by Dante Alighieri, but never Beatrice. Where love, of that kind, is reciprocal, it becomes the more destructively tragic: Antony, salt Cleopatra; Héloïse, and Abélard.

There is love, and there are loves, with a relation between them like that of the master's painting and the poor smudged print. And though I loved Kiri with such a wealth of torment as might make Hell itself admire, so daunting are the inadequacies of language that I have also to say I loved Alan, Carlitos —a little—and others besides, while now I love both Paul and Roderick.

For what I feel for Paul is surely not comprised in the word 'gratitude'? A bed may be shared with many a man, but when, sharing my bed, through weeks and more weeks a man has held me in his arms and stroked my damp hair till the cries of terror subside and the dream has gone, what I feel for him must overflow the banks of thankfulness. If, between us, there remain innumerable dry silences impossible to cover up, it is because when I am not crying out in absolute *need* of him, there is nothing, except thoughts, for either of us to give or take. The irritation he creates in me is with myself, no matter where it finds its vent.

*

It was never a secret when we returned to London together that both of us had bruises we did not wish just then to talk about. I do not think it was accepted then, nor have I accepted yet, that the nature of his wounds would never be revealed to me. Resentment may explain, then, why Paul has not been told the name of the person who taught me what self-portraits and looking-glass had never acknowledged: that I look ten years older than my age; why Paul still does not realise that the man too scared of the world's opinion to marry me was the Delphic Charioteer, Roddy the young and beautiful.

What relationship exists between them I have never understood. Hero-worship, on Roddy's side? A gruff benevolence, on Paul's? But then, I have never understood any of the relationships in which Paul participates: either what he feels for me and for Janice his wife, or what exactly has taken place between him and Celia.

Does Janice *mind* about my affair with him? The question sounds ridiculous. Of course and of course she must mind, if she is as other women are. There lies the enigma. Her Roman Catholic faith, the disease of which she is slowly dying, or her love of children would make her mysterious to me, even had she not asked Paul for a separation on the grounds that it would benefit their work! Helplessly I continue to lie with her husband, puzzle over what she feels, and postpone the day when I must go to her and ask. From her books, I suspect that she is not—unlike Celia—good.

*

Suppose that Celia was a stranger to me, if I had been informed that her favourite colour was pink I should imagine I understood everything about her. Knowing her, having borrowed her husky witching perfumes, I also know that her favourite painter is Piero, of the lucid intellect, and that I do not understand her at all.

When I came across that card I recognised at once who was the sender. Nobody else could have bought it to send at Christmastide in anything but blasphemy or jest. Joseph, a creeping bearded Shylock, casts a dubious glance at the Babe wound woodenly in swaddling-bands, who, balanced over her knobbly blue-clad knees, stares with bleary stoicism at His mother and receives a bleaker look back. Apart from the children at play across the purling river, the tiptoeing donkey, who wears no nimbus, is nevertheless the holiest creature present. 'Flight into Egypt', says the caption. 'From a book of Hours executed in Normandy about 1430–40.' And underneath : *With much love* (no signature) *to Paul.*

The idea that first came to me was the incongruous one that while I have very little capacity for abstract thought— not as little as Paul likes to suggest, but certainly not much— they had both read Greats. For a moment I felt blank; then it came upon me how funny it all was. To compete with a homosexual would be bad enough, but to compete with a philosophising saint!

The thought also occurred to me, not long after, that if the radiance was somewhat dimmed, the halo might have fallen askew.

*

It may be that the quality of love is known at the last less from its manifestations between the lovers than from what either or both will endure when it is withdrawn. Thus, while once it may have been the grossest lust, or pure, purest eroticism, mine has become that for which my children shall be born, no swing shall ever be hung in the wonderful garden, none of their voices shall ever freshly sound. A love of that kind may be worse than lust. It is also more complex, and more rich.

What became of my contemporaries, what happened to my friends? How sure and clever and swift they were, how keen, how biting, their minds! They were to govern the world: that was the purpose which shaped their education, gave their actions assurance, made lovely their poise; so that now—obscure schoolteachers, shabby dons, minor officials in minimal departments of the Civil Service; jailbirds, some, all with their edges gone and their reputations lost or unmade—when they find the world is run, as before, by the administrators they spurned, they suspect, shaken, the fault to be their own. Disillusion quietly crawls into the lines around the mouth; the eyes, once laughing, are uneasy; the smiles, increasingly perplexed. Novelist *manqué*; composer who somehow never met those necessary people; painter unable to understand the conventions of the avant garde; lecturer always deprived of his quested fellowship; brilliant student whose examination results were such a devastatingly *small* amount below what was expected of and by him . . . how difficult it is to remember their faces, and their names.

I too, what happened to me? Did I ever consciously learn to swim with the stream, or was it something more insidious that brought me 'success'—word grown ambivalent and two-edged on the taut mouths of my bitter shabby friends? For where is the painting, *the* painting, that would have justified the muddle of my life? Anne the wild one, Anne the unpredictable, what did I do to her, or when did she leave me, and where did she go?

Where is it now, the world I fought against, or the other world I hoped to win? What happened to Alan, stammering his profligate incorrigible way across three continents: in Paris an Apache dancer; singing in Stamboul; last heard of—gay illegible postcards—leaving from a Korean monastery for the mysterious 'Autonomous Region' (so says my atlas) north of Tibet, beyond the Kunlun Mountains. *I'll write to you again from Takla Makan. Why do you never believe in me?*

Oh, but I did!

He was nice, and he did love me in his own extravagant distinctly uncomfortable way. Once he proposed marriage, but since we were in bed at the time I thought he might have changed his mind by morning. Accept proposals before, perhaps, or after, with alacrity; do not accept proposals during the act of love. One sin at least, then, I never committed: helping him to become dreary too. Perhaps he is the redeeming person who remained what he was meant to be.

Oh, viewed from the outside my life is still not so very dull now; but viewed from inside it is shriekingly, screamingly dull. For what the hell is the use of being the mistress of a man who treats you as his wife—especially if you rather wish you *were* his wife?

Duologue two

They seldom breakfasted together. Next morning Anne confronted Paul in his study.

'You're not working?'

'Thinking,' he said. 'I'm tired.'

'Why don't you throw all those notes away and write your *book?*' she asked.

Rueful, he stared at the pile.

'Ah, men! You haven't the stamina for creative effort!' Anne said.

His retort was immediate. 'Why, what have women created?'

'Men,' said Anne promptly, 'and more women.'

'They don't do that unaided!'

'Do you suggest Michelangelo did the *Pietà* unaided?'

'I ask where there's any woman's equivalent of the *Pietà!*'

'Create the same conditions for women,' Anne replied, 'as for men . . .'

'There are similar conditions already!'

'There are not the *same* conditions, and you know it!'

'Example?' he teased.

Very well! Do you think if I, a woman, held an exhibition of paintings that consisted in its entirety of male nudes, the public would react in exactly the same way . . . ?'

'You wouldn't dare!'

'Would I not? But don't provoke me to something I might regret; that's not the point. There are certain things women are, by the common consent of *men*, allowed to do; everything else, they attempt at their peril. They may, for instance, write novels—*à la* Jane Austen: miniature, circumscribed, eminently ladylike, accepting all a lady's limits. . . .'

He moved, but did not speak. She waited a moment.

'*A la* Berthe Morisot,' she continued, 'women may paint. (And God what a betrayal there: you've seen the Manet portrait—that fiery gipsy face of hers—and you've seen her milk-and-water canvases?) *If* they accept the manner men allow them, women may compose. Fine. But what if a woman is so ungrateful as *not* to accept the limits set? What if a woman wishes to extend herself and the art she practises? Then a price has to be paid, and that price is, to be ignored. Men read the Brontës but don't write about them, just as they frequent prostitutes but don't attend their funerals. It's by mere chance, you think, that after all these years there's no standard full-length work on *Jane Eyre*?'

He reverted to the previous topic. 'If you should ever try to hold such an exhibition . . .'

'I'm talking of something else!'

'It doesn't interest me.'

'You're bloody rude! Can't we, for once, talk of something that interests *me*, instead of always *your* work?'

He made a quick painful gesture and she hesitated, evidently wishing to unsay it, but then went on: 'The Brontës were only published, even, because of the pseudonyms they adopted; otherwise, they'd have had to wait until their death.'

'The Brontës! They were just wild,' he said contemptuously, recovering.

'Do you say of a tigress that it's "just wild"? Yes, I believe you would! But do you say the same of the tiger?'

'Useful though it may be to the creature in gaining its

daily flesh, I hardly,' he said, 'view its wildness with unmixed admiration.'

It was now she who turned back. 'It enrages you that I might want to paint any male other than you, starkers or not; well, that's jealousy, an understandable failing. But it would enrage you more that I might wish to do a whole gallery of different male nudes—and that's a kind of vanity I resent because it debases you. You're angry because you suspect me, rightly, of being able, sometimes, to think about men as objects, paintable objects, chorus boys, just as you might in your male superiority think of women. And it's not that I might execute the wish, but that I possess it, that maddens you.'

'You're wrong,' he said shortly. 'I would just so much hate to see you make a laughing-stock of yourself.'

'Of myself? Or of you? Of you and your whole damned sex?'

'Anne,' he said. 'What is it? What is it that's going wrong?'

She suddenly asked him for a cigarette, though it was months since she had last smoked. 'I don't know,' she replied, as usual judicious, setting up an elaborate apparatus to examine the teeming mind. 'Maybe the old thing again : incipient insanity.'

'Don't, my sweet.'

'Incipient insanity,' she repeated. 'The beginning of madness. Why fear words?'

'Why exaggerate what are already horrors? You've over-come it before, and you can do so again—if necessary.'

'But *can* I?' she asked, nursing her arms to prevent the tremor from spreading uncontrollably. 'Can I, every time? How do I know that one day it won't beat me, hold me for ever in its clutch?'

He was suddenly helpless.

'You're right,' she said, comforting him. 'Absurd to exaggerate. After all, to have recognised the symptoms is . . . It can be stopped in time, perhaps.'

'What is happening in here?' he asked, running his hands gently across her forehead.

'Whispering,' she said quietly. 'At least—it seems not in here, you see, but outside, as though it comes from other people.'

'What is it you whisper?'

'Things about you and me. Often just repeating our names, or yours alone, but insinuatingly, and low. The intent is horrible, an accusation, not fit to be answered. . . . Don't worry,' she said, turning to him with a direct and smiling look.

'How can I not, when you leave me outside? And your work—you've not painted lately, have you? I noticed that. I don't like it when you only make sketches and brood. Is it another fallow period?'

'No—this time it's more, I think, like drawing breath before going on. The work has to come out of my present resources; I've plenty there.'

'You're sure?'

'If I were, there'd be no problem. No, I'm not *sure*, but I believe it's probably only a matter of learning to order my isolation.' She fell silent.

Then she cried, 'Would you thrust me screaming into the dark pit?'

Paul

If a man could pass through Paradise in a dream, and have a flower presented to him as a pledge that his soul had really been there, and if he found that flower in his hand when he awoke—Aye! and what then?

Samuel Taylor Coleridge, *Anima Poetae*

1

If, as Aristotle thought, 'it is in our actions—what we do—that we are happy or the reverse', what *do* we do? Anne paints, Janice writes, and both indubitably discover in their work (aware of it or no) the only happiness they are likely ever to possess. But is Roddy, because he teaches, a teacher? Is Celia a Civil Servant who gives away her superabundant wealth? And, trifler, dilettante, dabbling in archaeo-anthropo-socio-psychology, what am I (the 'lecturer in philosophy'), who annotate?

Time surrounds me as light does Anne, love does Celia, music Roddy, and people surround Janice. Each of our environments includes the constituents of all the others', but its emphases are different, and so its relationships. Time is the canvas Anne tries to cover with paint, the manuscript Janice covers with erasures and with words. Time is for Roddy a sequence of musical notations; it was once, for Celia, the shared delusion of those who could not face the eternal verities.

Clocks, calendars, revolutions of the earth and moon and

stars; writing-systems; languages; men, their gods and monuments—all are the same blind jester's playthings. Time is concerned with duration, and existence, and order, and progress, and events—'a mode of imaginative, as opposed to intellectual, thinking', according to one philosopher. To me it seems connected indeed with the imagination, but as module rather than as mode: a unit of measurement rather than a manner of measuring. It is the subject of my longest unwritten treatise.

To explain in retrospect a decision that was made in a sombre mood is difficult, the motives then usually being irrational. In such a mood I decided to write my doctoral thesis in Mexico and Guatemala; or, more precisely, to take for subject 'The Role of Time in the Mayan and Aztec Cultures'. I suspect it was the more trivial reasons which weighed with me most: for example, that I felt the fascination of the land where Montezuma was reluctant host to the Spanish adventurer Cortés, and the cruelties of two nations thus met.

I was perhaps lured especially by that strange story the Aztec emperor told, of how he and his people were brought to the country they now inhabited by a leader from oversea, the god-king Quetzalcoatl, who left them, and who would one day return from the waters of the East, leading an invincible army. At midnight a column of fire had been seen, all through the year; temples had been destroyed, by flame or silent lightning; a woman's voice cried, 'My children, we are lost.' Monsters appeared, to vanish immediately the emperor (was he mad?) had beheld them; an ominous bird was found, in its head a mirror of obsidian, or volcanic glass, which revealed the heavens, then a horde of armed men; and when the soothsayer arrived it flew away. Small wonder that when the white-clad Spaniards came with their magic weapons Montezuma displayed a compliance with the invaders' wishes so docile that he brought upon himself the ire of his own subjects, and was stoned by them to death!

'These buildings', said the prophecy, 'will become the homes of owls and wildcats, and all the grandeur of the courts shall cease.' So it came about; so, called now Cortés, Quetzalcoatl returned to his own.

*

64

I had always been inclined to make too many notes, and in Mexico, where there was so much to discover, it became an obsession. Eventually I had the material for three long books —to be written, I thought (or did I already know I should never write them?) in Guatemala. But it is not possible to bring anything to a conclusion in Guatemala. Anne, niggardly with excuses for herself and others, grants that excuse at least.

The light was bewildering, so pure and clear that it flowed. Torrential liquid gold fell on the city, and on the dazzling mountains. God knows what colour they were: blue, Celia said; but even if she was right, that was later. When first I came, and in the evenings pink traces of volcanic activity could still sometimes be discerned, I swear the mountains changed their aspect daily. Momentarily forgotten, they sprang up again whenever a corner was turned, and, purple, azure, grey, seemed inevitable.

At last I came across a little garden where work could be envisaged. I had already passed it once in the *camioneta*. It looked then scarcely two bus-lengths square, and so many people were strolling in it that I was not tempted to descend; but another day, after a long walk, feeling in need of rest, I unexpectedly reached it again. Once inside, I found that the garden could contain, in privacy, an extraordinary number of occupants for its size. It was so planted with trees and shrubs that children, students, tourists, vagabonds, lovers could all engage in their various pursuits with no discomfort to one another: there was shadow, and there was sun, there were variegations of the two; a diminutive fountain noiselessly sprayed, and there were fish, for anybody who cared to look.

I went there almost every day to work. The branches that screened me from the sky converted to indulgence what would otherwise have been necessity: staring at the hyacinthine heavens, overhead. The garden, with its ordered or apparently errant paths, its earth, and air, and water, and the occasional fire of cigarettes, became an image, in miniature, of my subject. Had I accepted the theories of Jung I might also have recognised in it a mandala or magic circle: a symbol of the self, the fountain central in the square, fulfilling yearnings for a harmony arduously won.

Time, I wrote, *for the Mayan and the Aztec cultures is not* linear, moving to a climax beyond history, but cyclical and circular, reflecting the revolutions of day and night, the hours, the seasons, governed by the sun—governed by the god of the sun, Humming Bird Wizard, whose death would end the present age, in earthquake end the world.

It was to ward off the world's end that the astronomy of the region was developed. Tutankhamen had charted the courses of the stars, and the Babylonians could predict eclipses of the sun, but for this, under the Maya, the calendar reached an accuracy unequalled, a thousand years later, by Pope Gregory. For this, zero was invented; for this were erected the stelae; for this, each day, each week, each year had their numbers, signs and patron deities. For this, in Uayeb, the month of five evil days that ended each cycle, fires were let out and all furniture was destroyed; pregnant women were locked into granaries lest under the influence of their nahual they be changed into wild beasts; and children were prevented from sleeping, lest they become possessed. For this were sacrifices made to Humming Bird Wizard: the most handsome, the bravest, captive was chosen, was taught the manners of a king; was shown how to play divine melodies upon the flute. Following the priests in procession, he mounted to the temple, at each of the steps breaking a flute. His body, in deference to his former godhead, was not flung, but carried, back down the steps after his head had been spitted on the rack provided for that purpose and, as the sun threw a shadow on the mid-point of the altar, his heart, with due ceremony, had been wrenched out.

Anne seeks reasons for what is done. Mine are for what would never be. Hunched, pedant, over notes in sundry cities, I ask myself why nothing reaches completion. The answer, as always, is a woman—several women.

2

The garden had a regular and a migrant population. Two people besides me frequented it habitually: a shambling vagrant with bent back, bearded mahogany face, rags that somehow suggested orange leather; and the girl.

The first week she was not there. After that she came every morning, towards noon, each time going straight to the fountain, where she stayed a short while, then immediately departed. Always it was as though the sun had gone in.

It puzzled me to decide her nationality. Her gracefulness and poise were unconscious—by her unvalued—and therefore not American; that she possessed them aroused doubts if she could be British; neither her golden colouring nor her sense of purpose were Latin.

Why, I wondered, was she always alone? Soon I could do no work before midday because I was awaiting her approach; when she had come I watched her; and when she departed, the cause of my presence was also gone.

Restless, I began to roam around the city and outside. One

Saturday I drove to Antigua, the old capital, meaning, if I liked the place, to take up residence there until my thesis was complete.

The inhabitants of Middle America now treat their religion prosaically, for all the plaster Madonnas and synthetic saints. A similar attitude seems to have affected their monuments, so that Antigua's churches impress by their age but never by their holiness. Whoever erected the notices, in bureaucracy's expansively courteous Castilian requesting the visitor not to urinate upon the floor, doubtless knew his people. I stared dutifully at cornices and corbels, or, with more enthusiasm, past devastated roofing to the sky, and hoped it would rain, to liven up my pilgrimage.

By the time I had walked to a smaller, honey-coloured church whose exterior was decorated with a white moulding of fruits and foliage reminiscent of the iced cakes with which the innumerable children of Guatemala celebrate their innumerable birthdays, it appeared more than probable that my wish would be granted, for dark clouds were draped overhead. Through musty pulsations of incense, I saw, peering in, an unprepossessing floral medley (saffron, white, with bunting, and flags), a glitter and glimmer from the altar, in honour, no doubt, of some putative virgin of the locality; so I strolled into the courtyard beyond, meaning to return only if prompted by a need for shelter.

It was powdered with the detritus of previous ages, and framed by dull pink walls. Like the

JARDÍN DE ISABELLA CATÓLICA

(whose name Anne for some reason always gets wrong), in the centre it contained a fountain; but its walks were unkempt, its flowers not cherished. Imagining the nuns who had lived there in times gone by would have been difficult. The falling water was all there was to see, and dry crumbling columns, a brass-studded door, broken archways, cells the haunt of spiders, were the sole memorials of former sanctity.

When I came back from reconnaissance, I saw the girl. She stood by the broad basin, gazing down into it so absorbedly that I could not help smiling.

And it began to rain. In Guatemala rain is sudden, tremendous, terribly chill. Looking around her with surprise, she seemed barely to understand what was happening; when she realised, she could still see nowhere to take refuge. As I hauled her unceremoniously after me, I saw what had captured her attention: for the walls, in those few seconds drenched, had become several shades darker, and, like Petra, were now a 'rose-red city "half as old as time" '—the same colour as the soaked stones of the basin must have been as she looked down into it, through the water.

'You wished to have the privilege of going to Tlaloc when you die?' I asked.

'To Tlaloc? What do you mean?' Her voice was like a bell heard through the golden smoke of dreams. 'I thought,' she commented, 'all the dead went to Mictlan?'

'It's not so simple. The east is for warriors, and the west for the women who die giving birth to them. Suicides go to the highest heaven. Those who die by water or lightning belong in Tlaloc's realm. But most of the rest, you're right, live with Mictlantecuhtli, if they can manage the journey between the mountains, over the desert and hills, and through the freezing wind that hurls stones at them—stones and obsidian knives. And if they can find the little red dog.'

'The little red dog?' she asked.

'To cross the river with, of course.'

'Like Charon?'

'Like Charon and Cerberus combined,' I agreed. 'You like water?'

'I love it.'

'Then will you come to the sea with me?'

She was laughing, even as she tried to be grave.

'But we haven't met,' I said, 'so you can't come with me to the sea, can you?'

'I think, in the circumstances, we count as having *met*,' she said, 'but everything is happening much too quickly.'

'Ah, you mean first we should talk about church architecture or something like that?'

She nodded, laughter dancing in her eyes. 'Why, for instance, did the Maya never discover the arch?'

'Because, I imagine, like the Egyptians and the Greeks, they kept their energy for higher things. Why have the Tibetans no word for non-sacred literature? Why have I never discovered God?'

'Have you not?' she asked.

'Have you?'

With a smile, 'I'm a missionary,' she said.

Anybody might fall in love with a prostitute, but the man whose *femme fatale* runs a mission, I superstitiously thought, must have done something to deserve what lies in store for him.

'You're forbidden to marry?' I asked.

'No, but I don't think I shall.'

'I think you people are utterly immoral,' I remarked.

She smiled again. 'But why?'

'You're going back to the city? Then I'll explain in the car.'

'Very well—thank you—if you can wait for me outside the church?'

We looked at each other, and she flushed. 'I mean while I . . .'

'Of course.'

*

A month later she came with me to the sea. The roads were bad; it was already night by the time we arrived. I ordered a meal to be prepared for her (soup, chicken, *frijol*) but myself did not have dinner. I supervised the unloading of *petates*—the green and brown palm-mats which, by the coast, take the place of beds—then munched a *tortilla* sprinkled with salt, and drank beer while Celia finished her coffee. I did not want to watch her choose where she would sleep.

'Celia,' I said, 'everything has been dumped higgledy-piggledy in one of the *ranchos*. Would you mind sorting things out? I'm going down to take a swim.'

When I returned, carrying the oil-lamp high, soft waves of song were coming from across the shore, where a group of youngsters chanted a Mexican ballad in competition with the wind and sea. Celia had spread out both *petates*, under the sheets and blankets, in the same hut, and was huddled in the far corner, clasping her knees, looking down at the smooth sand. Her clothes were in the *rancho* next door. I turned away and, dripping, searching for my towel, set down the lamp.

Then I extinguished it. Ashamed that I should already feel disappointed, in darkness I groped; my tongue found her mouth, my loins her thighs. She cried out, and with her pleading hands misdirected me.

In the morning I awoke first, at about five, and went down to the beach lest I should make love to her again. She had already swept and tidied the *rancho* when I came back.

As with the sleeping-mat in Japan, the *petate* is a module for the area and the height of the room; it would be hard to make anyone who had not seen them comprehend how harmonious the resulting proportions, and the clean soft colours of the woven palm-leaves, can be. I stood in the space that was the doorway, and contemplated Celia. The damp swimming-trunks clung to my body, and her eyes were timid, not knowing where to rest.

'You're too tall for your strength,' she said awkwardly, merely to disperse the silence.

Talking quickly to distract her attention from the evidence that my words were false, 'An unwound spring,' I said, 'with you. Usually, alas, I'm only too tightly coiled: the intellectual parasite, hunting prey. But easy prey, you understand.'

'Why are you so bitter?' she inquired.

'I think the real question is, Why are other people less bitter than I?'

'They want peace.'

I picked up the towel. 'Do you remember the conversation between Kate Leslie and Don Cipriano in *The Plumed Serpent*? He said war was no less natural than peace, and when she spoke of the other peace, that passes understanding, he didn't know what she meant.'

'What *do* you believe, Paul?'

'I'm an agnostic,' I said.

'Will you always say the same thing?' she asked, sighing. 'You've explained what you *don't* believe, but isn't there anything in which you do have faith?'

'Nothing at all,' I said, 'except when you are with me.'

She smiled.

'Come here.'

Very shyly she approached. I pointed to the sand. She lay

down beside me. Her fresh lips and her eyes, her husky voice, had all forgotten that she was a missionary, and the juices of her sweet body had never known. We awakened still together; my fingers twined in her hair.

'Paul,' she said, 'this is *wrong*.'

The tone was different from the one in which women usually say it. She pushed me, gently but decidedly, away. Angry, I persisted. War, I had to learn, was alien to her. She did not struggle. She remained completely inert.

Afterwards I was ashamed. We did not look at each other.

'I'm honestly sorry,' I said.

She arose, and rested her hand on my shoulder; then she knelt, passionately kissing me. 'When I said it was wrong I meant for me it's wrong, because that's how I feel it to be. I can't know what's right for you—but I'm sure not this. Even when we're married, to do it in this way would be wrong.'

'Only,' I replied, getting up, 'I'm afraid marriage isn't possible. There has never been any question of it.'

Her face turned the colour of ashes. Having dressed, I went over to the door and stood watching the sea. Yet thinking of her waiting there, still naked, with the blank golden eyes and the taskless hands, was worse than turning back and facing her.

'*Está la mesa!*' called the girl who served the large *rancho* where we ate.

'My wife is a Catholic, like you,' I said.

*

For the rest of the week, things were superficially the same. We slept together as before. We both knew it was over, not only from the sudden small eruptions, hints of the volcanic flaming beneath.

A ball thrown by a little boy landed at our feet once, in the sand. I tossed it back.

'You know the Olmec used balls made of rubber for their sacrificial offerings?' Celia said dreamily. 'It always reminds me of those beautifully naïve gifts in the Mystery plays—a bob of cherries and so on. I believe in one of them there *is* a ball.'

'Yes,' I said, 'you're exactly the sort of person who can never keep her mind on a single object, however tiny. You always, always, always have to be reminded of something else!'

'I'm sorry,' she said. 'What is it? What have I done?'

And seeing her flushed and ashamed, I took her quickly in my arms; I told her Janice was dying, we only had to be patient, one day we would be able to wed.

'Everything,' says Marcus Aurelius, 'is for a day, both that which remembers and that which is remembered.'

When Celia and I sleep in our separate graves there will be no one to remember, or forget, that my pretty little missionary, when first I took her, was not a virgin.

3

When the mission had been closed down and Celia was gone, I wrote to Janice giving my agreement to her proposal that we should continue to live apart. The plan was a formality, the embodiment of a suggestion originally mine, ratifying the *status quo*; yet I had felt unutterably hurt when Janice herself put it into words, and the mood in which I now gave my assent was one of punitive and masochistic rage. She was necessary to me. She was the excuse for my lack of achievement: with my jealousy of her work, what could I do? What could I do without it? What could *she* do? For I was equally necessary to her. She loved me, I am sure she loved me.

When, because of her failing health, our marital relations ceased, she begged me to take a mistress. 'My motive isn't,' she said, '*voyeurisme* exactly, though in my role as novelist I shall be interested to know your and her reactions, but that if I see you staring like a hungry dog I shall be horribly reminded of my own heat.'

'Is it *really* not possible . . . ?'

She gave her gusty laugh. 'Much as I should like to die in the act of love, my dear Paul, it would be an embarrassment to both you and my biographers. I'm serious about the mistress; it doesn't have to be anyone I approve of, but please, sweet, not a fool! You *need* criticism.'

She understood my terror of it, so strong that it may even have been the principal cause of my unwillingness to abandon my notes. Once complete a work, and what would hinder showing it to the public? How I shudder at Anne's caustic parodies of the reviews I occasionally did while teaching at Winchester!

Janice's own pungent criticism, no less rigorous, I had also wanted to escape. Being known as 'the husband of Janice La Bruyère', predictable fate for one who had married a woman novelist of some celebrity, was, on the whole, less irritating than the consciousness that, had she liked, she could have outranked me in my own terrain. Except—indirectly—unforgivably—through her comments on lectures of mine she sometimes attended, she shrank (always kind) from making that fact conspicuous. On the only occasion she approached my territory in print, she published under a pseudonym. Months later I came upon the article, as the result of a colleague's commendation, and recognised its authorship straightway, both from the subject (Babylonia) and from the familiar mandarin style. There followed an uncomfortable conversation with my wife in which both of us behaved as if I were charging her with having concealed a crime whose admitted perpetration she was to promise not to repeat.

*

The incident came immediately to my mind the day that, in a restaurant, I overheard two of our friends analysing with exact lucidity and undeniable compassion what they termed the 'failure' of our marriage—something of which I was hardly, till then, aware, and afterwards fought strenuously to reject.

' . . . poles apart,' said the first of the women, 'and unfortunately pretty cold ones, at that.'

'You think it's *his* fault, then?' the other mournfully asked.

'Fault? I didn't make the world; I'm not God (nor are you), to apportion blame. What's wrong with other people's lives is always so maddeningly easy to see, that's all. Take a long dry snake and a cuddly koala bear; arrange that the snake is the younger by some five or seven years; give the twinkling little koala heart disease; there you have Paul and Janice.'

'Don't you like Paul?'

'You think I dislike snakes? But I adore them! Need that prevent my realising that they're not the ideal playmate for Janice? I suspect the main trouble is that she looks on herself as a reincarnation of Colette.'

*

What is from the outside 'maddeningly easy to see' is nevertheless not necessarily so clear from within. The great goodwill between us, which keeps her door always open to me, was, paradoxically, what made it conceivable that Janice and I should separate with no grand inquisition.

'Our marriage was such a strange mistake!' she once said. 'I would have been the perfect Other Woman, for you; and then it would have been tragic, instead of only silly, that we can't make love together now.'

'Never mind,' I replied. 'You can still use either situation as a plot.'

Everything that can be said about the incomprehensibility of women applies with double force to those whose blood has received contributions from the French. It was the only time I saw her weep.

'I thought by marrying you I could frustrate the Other Man,' I said gently. 'But it never occurred to me I might be cuckolded by Death.'

She threw her pen at me and ordered me to leave her alone. Not understanding, I obeyed.

A marriage can survive many such bewilderments. Ours capsized not because of sudden squalls, a leak in the vessel, or a rising wind, but from commands not given, mismanagement, disaffection in the crew. One of us at least was uncertain why we had ever embarked.

Janice was older than I, and, I was given to understand, a widow: rich, not in need of security, with many friends. She had wanted, she said, children; but they died; and when we met it was, she said, too late. Her motive could only have been love, in marrying me?

Whatever my reasons had been when I proposed, to watch the slow, brave gaiety of her dying made my heart sore. It distressed and shamed me that already (though indeed with her encouragement) I was making plans that excluded her. The mistress she desired me to find would, she knew, become my second wife.

Perhaps what she most wanted was that I should start now on the way that would be mine after she had gone. Continuity pleased her; she disliked intensely the idea that the world was waiting with pent breath for the last rites to be administered and great changes to ensue. She would therefore dispose of all her possessions before that time—including, if need be, her husband.

Of the years the doctors gave her, most had now elapsed. It seemed that their prognosis had erred, if at all, on the side of optimism. The scare of six years before, when I was looking for an excuse to go abroad, was imminently due to be repeated.

'Egypt?' I had pondered. 'Or would it be too hot? Nobody's done very much on time and the early civilisations of America. . . . What do you think about Peru and the Incas, Janice?'

'Anywhere so long as you don't go to Guatemala,' she said briskly. 'Terribly dreary place; mules and revolutions, no proper roads. . . . One of my old friends runs a mission there, so I've read it all up.'

Did she really say that, or am I retrospectively inventing? A few days later, at any rate, I came across a book in her room, on the culture of the Mayas. 'Quite interesting,' she said, nodding at it. 'Awful place to be, though—guerilla warfare and what not.'

The idea was oddly attractive. I paid a visit to a travel agent and came home loaded with brochures—to find the doctor waiting for me, and Janice, blue-faced, confined to bed.

'Don't look so stricken,' she said when he had gone. 'It's a good time for me to cut the hawser, with you off to another continent.'

'The doctor says you mustn't talk,' I replied, 'and naturally I'm not going till you get better.'

'Paul,' she said derisively, 'do I look as though I shall get better? Let me have the luxury of chattering while I can!'

I did not reply. After a few days, however, her condition had very much improved, and she reverted, more imperiously, to her attempts to persuade me to leave. I spoke with the specialist. Eventually convinced, I left, a month later, for Mexico first, then Guatemala City.

Had my wife died then, I should have been free to marry Celia. Instead, the letter requesting a separation arrived the day that we returned, as lovers, from our week by the coast. I somehow could not bring myself to mention the news, or even compose, yet, my rejoinder to Janice. So often, in love, one dare not play the trump card, for fear it is not enough.

There was also something about my relationship with Celia that I found disquieting, though I could not then have explained what it was. When she had gone, I felt immense, inexplicable relief, despite my guilt and loneliness.

Loneliness hung all over the city. It was thickest in the little garden, which I could hardly bear to visit. No one except a few brawling children stopped at the fountain. The sky was bright. The water was still. The goldfish never appeared, nor the beggar with the imposing rags and face.

Almost decided to leave for the lowlands, *The Maya were alone among the peoples of Middle America*, I wrote, *in fixing a starting-point for the years of their calendar system. The date chosen as that point of reference is an obvious fiction, and probably connected with an hypothetical event.*

Just so, I shall always date everything from the year when I might have married Celia, of which the years are as numerous as the beans in a sack of cacao. How confusingly they mingle with those in which, when Janice dies, I must find the courage, or the ruthlessness, to propose to Celia indeed, uncertain of the answer she will give; and to discard Anne! Reality is so much less inevitable than any of our fond imaginings.

4

I waited a few weeks longer in the capital to see if any letter would come from Celia. There was none. I sent my luggage ahead of me back to England and travelled on a precarious aeroplane into the Petén, which it would be a pity, I thought, to miss after coming so long a way.

Sometimes one continues living only in case the activity might in the end regain the purpose it now lacks. Temples, museums, the people or plants or minerals around, then become a form of punctuation, pauses in the wearisome flow of cosmic insignificance. In the Petén, however, the insects flicked me into a state of irritation at least, much as a slight jolt will make the hands of a stopped watch erratically move again.

I found a place to tether my horse, and went to find the celebrated murals. All the figures I encountered were male: first delineated in red, then blocked in with areas of flat bright colour and finally outlined once more in black; I looked for female ones, to see if, as in Crete and Egypt, they would be painted yellow.

But the derelict temple was oppressive. Abandoning my quest, I quickly turned a corner.

'Oh! You startled me!' the woman said in English.

'I'm so sorry.'

'I was looking for the murals,' she said.

'In that case let me show you them.'

'But you were leaving.'

'Only because the place was so abandoned-looking.'

'Don't you like the solitude? There are more people here than where I've been, up in the mountains!' she said with a grin.

'You lived alone in the mountains? But there are bandits, they could have . . .'

'Yes, they tried to, once!' she answered derisively.

'You had a gun?'

'Oh, yes. I didn't want to use a gun at such close range, though—messy! My guardian taught me to drill lemons dead at twenty-five yards, but a human being three feet off is quite a different . . .'

'*Lemons?*' I interrupted.

'I can hit other things too, I'm no fetichist, but lemons were what I practised on,' she said.

'If you didn't use your pistol,' I demanded, 'what on earth did you do?'

'Twitched the *machete* out of his hand with the whip,' she replied, with a surprised, 'of course' intonation. 'It was only rape he was after, not money, so on realising I wasn't his sort he just loped off as he'd come.'

My expression must have amused her, for she laughed again. 'God, but your face is paintable. Hm—stand still a moment!'

'You're not by any chance Anne Rivers?'

'Yes, why?'

'I've always so much wanted to meet you. My name's Paul Hawkes. I heard you were coming here, but the Embassy couldn't give me your address.'

'No, I didn't register with them. *You* wrote that review of my London exhibition,' she said immediately. 'You're different from what I'd expected—I thought you'd be some awful queer. Does that sound rude? Really I'm tremendously grateful to you, you were the first person to take any proper notice of my work.'

By this time we were standing before the murals. Suddenly she shivered. 'I've had about enough of this country!'

'You're coming back to England? So am I. May I show you Mexico *en route*?'

'God forbid. I've seen it, thanks—all of it I can take!' She added, studying the murals more closely, 'At least the Maya aren't as cruel as the Aztecs.'

'No—curious, that, because they seem to have been just as indifferent to pain: they inlaid their teeth with jade, turquoise, gold and so forth, which must have been pretty agonising.'

'Ugh!' she murmured, then started. 'Heavens—mustn't miss the one and only plane—have you any idea of the time?'

'Which time? Julian, Gregorian, solar, Venus, *tonalpohualli*? The plane's due in an hour and sure to be late, we'll make it easily.'

'I *must* explore first! You go on, I'll catch you up.'

*

'One suddenly sees what Leonardo meant about the stains on damp walls as a source for art!' Anne exclaimed, swinging down from her horse.

Tremendously excited and exultant still, she took an enormous bite out of a green apple that she then thrust into her pocket. Her eyes were shining; she was not at all beautiful, but extraordinarily vivacious. As she absently gave the reins of her horse to someone who seemed to have been waiting for her, she saw me looking at her with desire. Immediately she went scarlet and did not know what to do, especially with her hands, so she reached for cigarettes, and, encountering the apple instead, stared down absurdly at that. The brilliant sun, sky, glittering grass and her streaming black hair became a poem by Lorca.

I kissed her; one of the muleteers, disconsolately idling without custom, yelled a sudden approving '*Olé!*' and when she turned to me, her cheeks still glowing, her eyes concerned and her mouth trying to express disapprobation, we both laughed for no reason, and her hand was already in mine as we entered the waiting aeroplane.

In Mexico I could not persuade her to venture past the nearest empty café. There under a pale round moon and a sky like milk, we sat talking. She asked for oranges, but instead I ordered green coconuts, green lemons, *tequila*.

> ' "*Nadie come naranjas*
> *bajo la luna lléna.*
> *Es preciso comer*
> *fruta verde y helada*", '

I said gravely.

'Lorca,' she said. 'Yes. "Nobody eat oranges under the full moon. What must be eaten are green and icy fruit." ' She sighed. 'How I shall miss the blood-coloured moon of Guatemala . . . burning pine branches, witchcraft, the warm raging sea!'

'You want already to go back?'

'Only,' she replied gloomily, 'because it's impossible.'

'Have you a home in England?'

'Neither in England nor anywhere else,' she said, but this time with a naughty grin. 'I like to play the female Byron.'

'That I had noticed.'

'I play it,' she said with sudden fierceness, 'to prevent discovering what's there when the act is over.'

'You've somewhere to stay tonight, at least?' I asked, rather amused, but committed to her beyond my wish.

She had withdrawn from me. 'Oh, there are places.'

'Like what? The Embankment?'

'Why not? It wouldn't be the first time I've slept there!'

'Doesn't anyone know you're returning?'

She shook her head.

'Come to my house, then, till you know where you want to go.'

'Thanks. Thanks very much.'

We went straight there on reaching London. Both of us were suffering from the feeling of disorientation that rapid air-travel seems to induce. When we had eaten, she fell asleep on one of the couches, I in an armchair; we both remained lazily supine long after we awoke.

'Come and help me unpack,' I said at last, and led the way upstairs. 'But first a bath!'

I went to turn the water on for her. When I re-entered the room, she was sitting thoughtfully on the bed. 'There are two bedrooms, I see,' she said questioningly.

'Yes, there are. But please sleep here. That's what you want to do?'

She sighed softly, with the relief of one no longer lost, and told me, laughingly yet with curious tenderness, of the remark Carlitos had made to her: 'You are not afraid.' Nothing could have more absurdly travestied the truth.

That first night, when, awakened more by the suddenness of her movement than by any sound, I discovered her standing perfectly still in a dark room downstairs, I myself became for a moment involved in the nightmare of her terror.

'You're often sleepless?' I asked, switching on the light.

'Dreams wake me, and then I daren't go back to bed.'

'Is it always the same dream?'

'The same dreams—there are several—yes. They call it "perseveration", don't they: the same posing of a problem to which there is never any solution one can accept?'

'Would you like to tell me what it is?'

'What's the use? In real life there's no solution, and you couldn't explain any more of the dream than I already understand myself!'

'Then may I give you a drink, at least?'

'Having spoiled your sleep, I *ought* to explain!' she said ruefully. 'Well: one of the dreams starts with a . . . reptile . . . I find on the floor. The body is a snake's; the head is like a wood-louse, rounded and blunt. At first, in the dream, I am paralysed with revulsion. Then I carry the creature to the lavatory and flush it away—always apprehensive in case it won't go down. It goes all right. After that, either there's a rest from dreaming, or part of my mind acts as censor so that when I awake I can't remember what intervened. The next bit, anyway, seems to have no connexion: I am in bed with someone whose face I can never recall afterwards but whom in the dream I know to be my brother.'

'You make love?'

'Yes,' she said, 'we make love, and I feel ashamed, but he behaves as if our conduct is customary, expected. And then there's a switch to the wood-louse/snake again, all as before except that this time when I pull the chain the creature doesn't go away. At that point, I awake.'

'Why didn't you put the light on in here?' I asked.

'In case—I know it's not rational, but in case it was in the room.'

'And if it was, you'd prefer to be with it in darkness?'

'God, God!' she cried. 'Stop it, stop it, please!'

'How do you interpret your dream?'

'The snake is the sexual act,' she said more coolly. 'My conscience is suggesting to me that I ought to refrain; in the first part of the dream I accept that suggestion. The wood-louse may mean the act for some reason is contemptible to me—or, since having a louse's head makes the snake fangless, perhaps I'm already arguing against my conscience, and saying "But this doesn't do any harm!" ' She hesitated, and then said : 'Only at the same time the revulsion I feel is more for the wood-louse than the snake.'

'And how do you explain the incest?' I prompted. 'What are your relations with your brother in real life?'

She laughed. 'I have no brother.'

'Oh! And you've never experienced any conscious shame with your lovers?'

'On the contrary,' she said. 'The sexual act brings me a spurious peace.'

'The interpretation you give isn't the only possible one,' I observed.

'The lavatory could represent the uterus or the vagina, you mean? There are countless interpretations. The whole of the reptile part could be fear that my lover might become impotent; but that hardly fits the facts of my life. Why should I fear an impotence I've never encountered? The "brother" may be standing in for someone,' she went on, as it seemed retreating from the subject introduced : 'a friend, maybe. This is the part I can't work out satisfactorily. Or he may denote my *animus*, the male half of my personality. In either case he is saying, "It's all right, there's no need to be ashamed or afraid." '

'And in the last instalment you are announcing that even if you should abstain as your conscience suggests, the urge would still be there?'

'Yes—abstinence is no solution. Not for me.'

'When did the dreams start?' I inquired.

'Why, about . . .' She stopped, and a look of surprise crossed her face. 'Quite a long time ago,' she said with finality, and, abruptly turning, went through the dark hall to the staircase. Halfway up, she changed her mind, and said with a sudden peal of laughter, 'Very soon after the end of my last affair. Oh, heavens, is it as simple as that?'

In our room I poured out whisky for us both. She left most of hers.

'You'd hardly need a louse-headed snake to convince you that life is pleasanter with its sins?' I asked.

'Perhaps not,' she idly agreed. Looking at the photographs on the wall, 'You're married, aren't you?' she remarked.

'Yes,' I said.

'And your wife is Janice La Bruyerè?'

'That's right. We've been separated, though, for a couple of months now.'

'Is that why you're unhappy?' she asked.

'No,' I replied, 'the wish for a separation was shared.'

'Equally?'

'I suppose not. It would be difficult to say.'

'You don't mind my asking you?'

'No, go ahead,' I said. 'I've been catechising you, God knows!'

'You'll obtain a divorce, then?'

'I can't,' I said. 'Janice is a Roman Catholic.'

She nodded.

'You've read her books?' I asked.

'Yes. But that's not how I knew she was your wife. She used to be . . .' (the hesitation, which I had encountered in other people, was this time very slight) 'a friend of my guardian.'

'Stephen Farmer?'

'Yes,' she said with deepest gloom. 'This awful inbred society of ours, where everyone knows everyone else!'

'Not quite everyone. But they do all seem to connect up in the end.'

85

'How many years before you could bring an action on grounds of desertion?'

'As I agreed to let Janice go, in this case technically there is no desertion.'

'But supposing you asked her to return, and she refused?'

'That might in certain circumstances constitute a ground for divorce, but one couldn't in all humanity divorce a dying woman! What's more, if I asked her to, she would undoubtedly return—and divorce is no use to me, anyway.'

'Forgive me. I jumped to the wrong conclusion. I thought you had a rather fettered look.'

'If I'm fettered, it's not by my wife.' I picked up my glass. Indicating the contents of hers, 'You've decided to abstain from *everything*?' I asked.

'No. Make love to me again, make love!'

But when it was over, she cried, because, I think, of her enjoyment, which was to her a greater betrayal than the mere act of faithlessness.

'Will you be able to sleep now?' I asked, when the sobs had changed to her customary self-directed mirth.

She nodded.

'Do you have other nightmares?'

'Yes, there are several. There's one involving a pond of fish, but I know what *that's* about.'

'Perhaps they're all connected?'

'Perhaps.'

*

Anne's unconscious involuntary demands, the wishes she voiced and those she would not utter, depleted my vitality to such an extent that I was almost relieved when she submitted herself for treatment at a hospital for nervous disorders, and more than angry when shortly after, against her doctor's advice, she left.

'I don't understand why you did anything so foolish.'

'No, you wouldn't,' she said curtly. 'The sight of people waylaying the nurses to try to get their ration of drugs before time would be demoralising even if one was well. If I'm to become addicted to dope I can do it in more comfort outside.'

'But tranquillisers . . .'

' "Tranquillisers", drugs, dope—I don't care what tag their pills and potions are given.'

'I hardly see why you should consider alcohol so much more admirable!' I said, irritated by her rudeness.

'For one thing it *tastes* better than bloody peraldehyde! But the whisky cure was your idea,' she answered, truthfully enough, 'and, as such, one I can do without!'

Alcohol and cigarettes were given up in the same day.

Uncomfortably I watched, meaning, the moment her state showed signs of aggravation, to persuade her to use anything that would make it more tolerable; but to my surprise it soon seemed to have improved.

'The dreams have stopped?'

'Yes. They've been replaced,' she said wryly, 'by thought-blockages: a labyrinth, in which I keep losing the thread. The basic trouble is that I don't *want* to be normal!'

'But no one has any desire to condemn you to the kind of life other people might find normal. The thing to discover is only what is normal for you.'

'I've got myself into scrapes always.'

'Then we must find out what is your normal sort of scrape,' I retorted.

'I do so hate being dragged into people's splendid teams,' she said with a sneer. 'Whom do you mean by "we"?'

'You, then, if that's what you prefer,' I said, discouraged and fatigued.

'I'm sorry, Paul. When I'm in this mood I snap at every-one.'

She came over to me. I nodded and went out of the room, leaving her standing awkwardly in an attitude of unkissed contrition.

*

So we continued, with quarrels followed by apologies which were as often as not rejected, and brief lulls during which all her symptoms disappeared, only to be replaced by new ones, of which the latest, and most alarming, were auditory illusions, ideas of reference: a paranoid mishearing of conversations so that she interpreted them as criticism of her own (and sometimes, in conjunction, my) behaviour. Frequently I wondered if her instability was an attempt to bring about the cessation of her work, and whether, that being so, she differed from Roddy, Celia, Janice and me only in finding it harder to stop, than to continue, working. What I did by toying with notes, Celia by closing the mission, Janice by agreeing to die, and Roddy by taking a job to which he was hopelessly unsuited, Anne might seek to do by imitations of neurosis? At other times, perhaps by projecting my own anxieties upon her, I felt the true solution would be for her more fully to accept that she, like all the rest of us, was mentally as well as physically bisexual.

5

If asked about my motives in electing to teach at Winchester, I should have to admit my prime reason was that I wished to acquire the manner, without the commitments, of a Wyke-hamist. Physiognomy aided me in this: all my lineaments seemed to have been applied something too low and too far forward on the face, leaving me with the typical high flat forehead, menacing nose, crisp thin mouth and abbreviated chin. I cultivated a clear, clipped delivery in my speech; my style of exposition had the authentic disdainful colourless-ness.

By some instinct for the correct, the commendable, choice, I taught Classics: a fact which combined with various acci-dents to secure my nomination for the office of housemaster at an age so early that it was plain I should have to shift quarters if my career was not to end at the stage already close; but, being of a temperament inimical to change, I loitered and doddered and faltered.

Had I not done so, would I ever have become involved

with Roddy? And, not meeting Roddy, would I still have married Janice, still gone to Guatemala, still loved Celia, and still lived with Anne?

Unphilosophical speculations! The past is fixed, and if existence is to be looked on as no hypothesis, but very actuality, the roads taken are the only roads, the doors thrown wide the only doors.

I met Roddy, then, and fled. I fled because while I can accept with equanimity that every man comprehends certain female elements and every woman is partly male, when I meet the person who makes those circumstances ones I have to contend with every day and fight in horror to restrain, my impeccable instinct advises retreat. I retreated from Winchester with discretion, and into marriage with more haste than virtue. A proposal was made to me that put a lectureship and the hand of a wealthy woman within my grasp. I accepted it. Our honeymoon was spent in Venice, where I admired the Canalettos, and my wife the *gondolieri*.

I sensed the disturbing features in her before I knew how to name them; nor would I guarantee to have learned their names yet. At first sight no woman could have appeared more amiable, more yielding, more bland than this little koala of the twinkling eyes. One's next discoveries served not to obliterate but to enrich that impression : she had a foreign and an exotic scent about her, an allure, an enticing charm, as of sandalwood, or myrrh. Only gradually, by breaths, and hints, and perfumed sighs, did it emerge that there was an infrangible hardness somewhere at the core. To me she became in time not koala, but squirrel guarding winter hoard; and the mirrors with which she surrounded herself no emblems of frail feminine vanity, but useful warnings of an intruder's approach.

I was not accustomed to dealing with women of an analytical turn of mind, and when the thought came to me that my wife, for all her apparent relaxation, must merely on the evidence of her books have an extraordinarily vigilant eye, I found it exceedingly unpleasant. Janice detected my discomposure. Nothing was ever put into words. We continued as before, except that from then on I played, albeit soberly, with plans for escape, until at last the beautiful simplicity of separation occurred to me; or was put into my head.

For that too was disturbing : the number of projects regarded as mine which on examination were found to have their origin in some observation made by my wife.

The bed-ridden see not only from a different angle, but at much greater depth. That there inheres a relation between Proust's cork-lined room and the profundity of his vision seems to me indisputable; and if my wife's illness is likewise up to a point *voulu*, I cannot censure her for having divined what situation would profit best her pen.

Is it cruel to suppose that Janice bears at least part of the responsibility for her own cardiac disease? I do not single her out in any way; in my opinion we all, later, or sooner, *consent* to die, and those live longest whose hold on life is the most stubborn. When we believe we shall die, we have begun to do so.

In like manner, then, Anne could be held to account for her own disorders of the mind? I believe, in part, she could. When her condition has reached its nadir, no one would think to blame her, because the pain of it is visibly immense; but for the progress towards that pitch of pain she would herself accept some responsibility (even, perhaps, with pride). But the question is a perplexing one. By the time any human being has attained full consciousness of what he is doing— for which he needs experience—he has already, unless he possesses singular innate virtue or a good fortune not of his own workmanship, made several, or many, mistakes; and those mistakes must diminish his awareness and responsibility. On finding oneself in the dark wood one tends to go forward rather than back; what errors have been committed are past, one thinks, not seeing how they may shape the future. And 'forward' means little more than 'in the direction in which my face happens to be set'.

Is Roddy at fault for having chosen his present career? Again the issue is complex. What Stephen intended when he counselled his son not to go to Sandhurst I can only surmise; he may very well have been right. It is possible that the boy himself, when he decided to become a schoolmaster instead of continuing to practise, as well as to study, music, may have had the most praiseworthy motives. If he was himself cognizant of the tendencies I impute to him, to avoid a world he no doubt thought of as long-haired would have been at the least eminently sensible; and the death of his father probably made it necessary that he should adopt a role less precarious, whatever his wishes, than the composer's one.

Unfortunately no subterfuge quite disguises my sneaking belief that what draws me to Roddy is his absolute corruption —the same quality, I suspect, that holds Anne in thrall to him. There is something about that patrician face, that suggestion of a brilliance deliberately darkened, that stiff refusal to move, even if only to receive advancing worshippers, which fascinates us both.

Whether I was attracted to Celia for herself or for her reminiscences of Roddy I can never ascertain. Neither am I convinced that Anne's desire for Roddy is pure of all alloy. These problems must remain unfathomable as the question of who took his sister's virginity—another on which I possess my unsupported views.

I hardly know whether my fancy that we are all five of us devoid of happiness is any the more susceptible of proof. Anne affects to consider both Roderick and Celia happy; in the latter's case I know her happiness was what I feasted on till none was left.

*

When I made a facetious attempt once to congratulate her upon her intellectual reawakening, she said, 'I've forgotten the meaning of love.'

'Isn't this love?'

'Love's shadow, it seems to me.'

'Aren't you happy?' I asked. 'I mean, don't you have any pleasure with me?'

'That's just the trouble! Don't you remember Plato said the realities must be painful at first?'

'To those who have been in the dark cave . . . Yes, but suppose here where we are is paradise, where you *were* was the cave of illusions, and what you think of as conscience is the pain of seeing the light?'

I could not convince myself, let alone her.

*

Am I happy? I am not.

Have I ever been happy? I think I have, without knowing it at the time; but I may be making the very same fool's mistake as is reaffirmed from every prize-giving platform in the land to an audience of bored, scrubbed, sullen or beaming children: 'Your schooldays are' (whereas they should say, 'will have been') 'the happiest days of your life.' Happiest, that is to say, in being irrecoverably past: we may fall in love again, break a leg again, re-marry, lose our fortune again, but we shall never go through infancy again, or the purgatory of childhood.

And will I be happy tomorrow? Tomorrow, yes, beatifically! but before tomorrow comes it turns into today, and today is terrible.

For Janice, in her dying, and for Celia, in her loss of faith; for Anne, in her fear of madness, and for Roddy, who has found no love but her he spurned in youth, today is terrible. But the yesterday that was today is worse.

Janice, of us all, must be the closest to happiness. Time takes much, but gives more. It will take the squirrel eyes and the neat dark hair; it will eradicate the putrefying flesh that was my wife, but it will offer to her private grave the clean bone. When darkness has been brought her, she will need no drugs for sleep. Softly it will woo and win her with caresses, and in its embraces she will experience eternal felicity, the felicity of slumber, the felicity of unconsciousness, the felicity of Nothingness, rapture's pinnacle and height. We shall envy her then her death.

I see not only the mistakes we have committed already, but those others we shall surely make. When Janice, Celia's heroine, dies, the memory of all the abandoned beggars will return. When Janice dies, there will be decisions to make, for us all; but are any of us capable, except in theory, of making new choices in a situation we have faced before? Have I the audacity to propose to Celia? Has Roddy the courage to propose to Anne? And if we had, would Celia, or would Anne, accept?

Duologue three

'Anne, darling! What dark pit?'

'Is that what I said?' she asked heavily. 'I don't usually get quite so carried away by my subconscious urges!'

'Will you be all right if I leave you, a moment, so as to make a pot of coffee?'

'Yes, yes. Yes, please do that. Please do that.'

'Anne! Pull yourself together!'

She looked up. 'I'm all right. Go on, make the coffee.'

'There's nowhere I would have you thrust,' he said when he returned. 'Neither the dark pit nor anywhere else. I want you here with me.'

'I know. I'm just a bit tired.' Anne leaned forward to spoon sugar into his cup. 'What are you writing about?'

'Pain,' Paul said, 'and cruelty.'

'In general, or . . .?'

'As usual, particularly the Maya and the Aztecs.'

She sipped the hot coffee. 'What conclusions have you reached?'

'You ought to know I never reach a conclusion!'

'That was my way of suggesting that you should! What hypotheses, then, have you started from?'

He tilted back, biting the cap of his fountain-pen. 'I'm wondering how far the impression of cruelty is due to the recalcitrant materials they used.'

'The Aztecs?'

'Late Mayan is rather cruel too; they degenerate; but mainly the Aztecs, yes. Obsidian is so hard; everything done in it has open or latent cruelty.'

'But the Aztecs didn't invariably use obsidian?'

'The things that remain in the mind are always obsidian, rock crystal, jade—hard, refractory, all three.'

She considered. 'Yes, or flint. But what about that maize goddess in Copán . . .?'

'Limestone,' he said briefly, 'but Early.'

'Well, it *is* another material, and the occurrence of other materials shows your Maya and your Aztecs had a choice; if the cruel things are the most memorable, it only reflects their tastes—and, of course, one's own. No,' she decided, 'I agree with Modigliani, who said the stone makes very little difference: the feeling of hardness or softness comes from the sculptor, comes from within.'

'However he ranks as a painter, Modigliani's sculpture isn't much to back an argument with.'

'That doesn't disprove his theory,' Anne objected.

'But it gives you nothing to help prove it. I grant your point about the limestone, though there wasn't much of that available. You're smoking again?'

Defiant suddenly, 'Yes, and drinking too,' she said.

He lit their cigarettes.

'Your opinions on art are much more self-consistent than those you hold on morality,' he said curiously. 'You always claim that there's no objective reality—that reality is what the artist chooses to make it; and yet, about ethics, about morals, you say . . .'

'I've never claimed anything of the kind!' she tartly interrupted. 'My argument is that not reality, but the interpretation of it, is subjective; and the interpretation, being a kind of metaphor, may introduce a new reality. But go on.'

He took a moment to retrieve the thread. 'While you hold that saints objectively exist, I was going to say, you seem sometimes to suggest that they're born, and sometimes that they're made. And . . .'

'No. I merely believe that saints are so only in retrospect—rather like Solon. "Call no man happy till he dies." If choice is really open, no matter what the background is our next choice might suddenly be evil and wrong; yet I can't help feeling that if each previous decision has been right we stand a better chance of making the right choice this time and the next.'

'The saint, to you, is just the person who makes the right decision always?'

'The born saint, yes: the irritating kind who's difficult to respect or feel any affection for, who "never sets a foot wrong". But the made saint discovers the right choice only in the teeth of his own temptations; he may commit a thousand sins, a million errors, but eventually he wipes them out by his martyrdom—which may be physical *or* spiritual; or even, I suppose, mental.'

'There's no room for grace in your scheme of things?'

She paused, and defiantly rallied. 'No. Perhaps that's it. There's no more room in my scheme of things for grace—only for will-power.'

'Forgive me if I say you're arrogant!' he exclaimed.

'Forgive me if I say I knew.'

'Complacent, then, besides!'

'Arrogance and complacency are both things I fight against!' she protested.

'How do you know your "born saint" hasn't as grim a struggle?' he inquired.

'I infer it,' she responded, 'from the absence of carnage.'

'By carnage you mean depression?'

'No, I don't as a matter of fact. Most of the born saints seem to me not only as depressing as all hell but pretty depressed themselves too. By carnage I mean signs of the struggle.'

'Perhaps the depression is a sign.'

'Then is the struggle worth it?'

'To them, or other people?'

99

'To God,' she said demurely. 'He ought to matter most. Read me a riddle, Paul, while we're on this subject?'

'Very well, what is it?'

'The egoist is concerned above all with himself, yes?' she proposed.

'That, Socrates, is true.'

'And egoism is generally accepted to be wrong?'

'I believe it is.'

'And God is saying to us, if we could only hear Him, "Love not yourselves, My children, but Me"?'

'That is what those who believe in Him assert.'

'Just as each one of us says, "Love not yourselves, but me"?'

'Well, not exactly,' he said.

'Not?' she asked. 'What is the difference, please?'

'I appreciate your point; but that,' he said, 'is something I should have to think about.'

'Yes, Paul.'

'Every concept of God so far evolved is more or less anthropomorphic.'

'Then wouldn't the first step towards a truer creed be to discard or destroy all the existing concepts?'

'Possibly; but how would you set about doing it?' he asked.

'I?'

'If you want to find God,' he said.

She gazed around the room. 'Do I want to find God?'

'If you don't know, I can't think who else would!'

'God himself, maybe? No; I don't believe in destruction, until you've seen what you can make.'

'You really can be one of the most annoying women I've ever met!'

'Have you met many annoying women?' she asked innocently. 'Now, a person I always find intensely annoying is our friend Celia.'

He got up.

'What's the matter?'

'Nothing's the matter,' he said. 'I want some more coffee, that's all.'

'Do you think you ought to have any more, if you're still a bit edgy? You do? Then let me pour you some.'

'Why don't you like Celia?' he demanded suddenly, grasping the cup.

'There's no sugar in that,' she observed.

He reached savagely for the bowl.

'Haven't you put too much, now?'

'I said,' he repeated rigidly, 'why don't you like Celia?'

'I like Celia very much. That's why I introduced you. And I ought to be awfully grateful to her, oughtn't I, her father having been my guardian? Paul, do throw that away and take another cup!'

'It's perfectly all right like this,' he said.

'You're very adaptable!'

'Is taking one extra spoonful of sugar such a calamity?' he asked.

'I should have thought three large spoonfuls must be fairly unpleasant for anyone who prefers two small. But I'll encourage you in your stoicism if you wish, I'm sure it's highly admirable.'

Moving abruptly to replace on the table his cup, he spilt some of his coffee into the saucer.

'Dear, dear! That's what violence does for you.'

'I wish you wouldn't say "Dear, dear" like that!'

'Yes, isn't it exasperating?' she agreed. 'Especially when one's nerves are a little bit strained. And so out of character! I must have caught it from Celia when she was here the other night. As *she* says it, it sounds sweet. It's a pity she's not here now; she always likes to take three large spoonfuls of sugar. You wouldn't like me to drink what's left of that?'

Goaded beyond endurance, he thrust back the table and made for the door.

'Ah, I see you're late for your lecture—I shouldn't have kept you talking. And you didn't have time to finish your coffee after all. What a shame!'

She tapped into a stack the notes he had forgotten, presenting them to him expressionlessly when he turned. The door slammed after him, and she gave a slightly guilty grin.

Celia

¡Felicidad! no he de volver a hallarte
en la tierra, en el aire, ni en el cielo,
  aun cuando sé que existes
  y no eres vano sueño.

Rosalía Castro

Happiness, I shall never come to find you again
on earth, in the air, nor in the sky,
  in spite of knowing that you exist
  and are not a futile dream.

1

There is a fine broad road across Zone 5 of Guatemala City, embellished with clean, modern garages whose gay bunting twirls frivolously in the wind. Thrown down anyhow like a pack of old disused playing-cards, and giving off the same pathetic air of cheap unimportant vice, on the slope at its side as the bus travels through La Palmita towards the cinemas of Zone 1 hundreds of shacks are tumbled together, precariously balanced at crazy angles. People, Indians, live in them.

'We have no colour problem,' every Guatemalan will proudly tell the curious visitor. Perhaps they are right. Perhaps the Indian is not treated differently *because* he is brown. But the Indian *is* brown, and he *is* treated differently—not undernourished, perhaps, so much as starving.

The colour problem (male and female) is sitting on the pavements with a begging-bowl and an outstretched hand. The colour problem (male) has typhoid instead of drainage, and his children's play-pool is filled with human excrement. The female colour-problem rises at six in the morning and goes to bed 'when she has finished her work'—that is, at ten or eleven at night, with three hours' holiday on a Sunday evening and a reprimand when she returns late.

'The city has very attractive residential quarters', says the leaflet one of the European airway companies hands out to its passengers. Such quarters, new, glistening, are to be found, for example, near the Palacio Nacional and the Embassy of the United States of America in the centre of the city, and near the house of the Guatemalan President, in Zone 10.

'For night-life,' the leaflet continues, 'there are several good bars and night clubs where you can dance to typical Marimba-orchestras.' There is also the red light district in Zone 5.

Whereas the sleazier parts of London exude a furtive fever, an atmosphere of barely contained excitement, here there is only boredom. Soho has its shabby intent dreams and dreamers, but in the *barrio rojo* of Guatemala there is neither dreamer nor dream. The brothels are licensed, and their doors stand wide open while clients are admitted; the beds are visible from without. A few men stand around with their backs to those open doorways. They are not ponces or bouncers. They are not waiting for, or interested in, anyone. They have no money, but they do not seem from the expressions on their faces to be thinking about that. From the expressions on their faces they do not seem to be thinking about anything. All of them are apathetic. Some of them are young. The prostitutes too are apathetic, and some of them are young. Syphilitic, Lesbian, trafficking in drugs, they come from Cuba and Puerto Rico, from Haiti, from Honduras, from Trinidad. The price for the use of their human flesh is one dollar for a 'short time', or five dollars for the night.

Three thousand years before the birth of Our Lord there was a maize agriculture in this land, developed out of the wild grasses. Transport was by water or on men's backs. Social unity was imposed from ceremonial cities rising magnificently out of a hot and humid jungle which had incessantly to be cut back with stone tools and which incessantly encroached again upon the areas cleared. In an insect-ridden wilderness the tallest pyramids in the world were erected: with a Stone Age technology; without the use of animals; and with no help from the wheel.

Into this peasant people, who possessed gold and valued jade ornament more highly, who were armed with glass swords, wooden clubs, and chips of stone, rode the forces of Pedro de Alvarado, most ruthless captain of unmerciful Cortés, bringing with them not only metal armour, and gunpowder from Popocatépetl, but a variety of diseases—syphilis, small-pox, yellow fever—against which the Maya had manufactured no biological defence. In the name of God, St James and Spain, elaborately chased golden vessels, bought for a handful of cacao beans, or requisitioned like the women, were barbarously melted down for shipment to the coffers of the emperor Charles V.

This was the beginning of the foreign exploitation from which Guatemala has suffered ever since; and perhaps, of them all, despite the cold atrocities of Alvarado, the Spanish record is the least sorry. It is to be doubted, furthermore, whether the inhumanity of foreign powers has been appreciably greater than that of the indigenous *ladino* dictators.

When I had gone over most of the city on foot and the rest by bus, I stared at the mountains, remembering all that Anne had ever said about the charity of blundering fools, and I went up there alone for a while to study the history of the land. After forty days and forty nights, when I had prayed the anger out of me, I came down once more; and behind me the shining mountains were blue as the Madonna's robe.

*

The situation of the mission centre indicated clearly what the first problem would be. I entered, introduced myself to the servants, and was shown into the presence of the other missionaries, three in number, who were at lunch.

Preliminary exchanges over, 'We hardly expected you to be so young!' squeaked the pale man with the goatee.

I smiled at him. 'My predecessor was much older?'

'Sixty-four when she, ah, ah . . .'

'Died?' I said.

Looking reproachful, he nodded. 'To the world, Miss Farmer, to the world.'

'But you're not taking any chicken?' said the middle-aged woman.

'Thank you, no.'

'*Do* take some chicken?'

'No, thank you.'

'You're a vegetarian, Miss Farmer?'

Then here the fight must begin. 'Unless or until the general standard of living in the capital improves, I don't intend eating chicken. This is a mission, and I'm a missionary.'

The consternation on her face changed gradually to outrage. 'Do you expect us all to follow your example?'

'I don't know whether you intend to stay.'

'Is that a threat, Miss Farmer?'

'Excuse me,' the younger of the men said mildly, 'does anyone really think this is the time to . . .'

'The rest of you have finished lunch,' I said, 'and I should prefer things to be clear from the start. I would like to tell you now that I am already planning to transfer this mission to another neighbourhood.'

'But—Miss Curtis, Mr Baines!' the goatee rallied them. '*Here*, we're so close to . . .' He hesitated.

'The shops?' I suggested. 'The restaurants? The cinema?'

'Where,' Miss Curtis suddenly demanded, as no one seemed inclined to reply, 'are you moving us to?'

'To Zone 5.'

'Zone . . .?'

'Zone 5,' I repeated.

'Miss Farmer,' the goatee interposed gently. 'You are a stranger here, and probably you don't understand. Zone 5 . . .' He cleared his throat.

'Is the place where the prostitutes live,' I supplied, 'and the children of the prostitutes. Our job will be to help them.'

'Those who touch pitch . . .' began Miss Curtis ominously.

'I can imagine no part of the city where it would be easier to be defiled than at this address.'

'You're serious?' the young man asked.

'Yes.'

'I hoped for a moment you had a sense of humour. Well: with great regret, I for one will be leaving you.'

At times, pomposity too has its place. 'God will make the final decision, Mr Baines?'

'There is no need to be blasphemous, Miss Farmer,' said Miss Curtis stiffly. 'There are some situations too absurd for prayer. I should like to warn you now that I shall complain to your superiors.'

'You will find that complaint is of very little avail. Tomorrow morning, by the way, I wish to go through the accounts with you.'

She turned red.

'Do I take it that all three of you are leaving?' I asked.

Conferring by glances, they nodded.

'And,' Miss Curtis tartly added, still red, but indomitable, 'it might be better if we took our meals separately, to avoid friction.'

'You may, of course, eat when and where you please,' I said. 'The food served here will be simple, and the servants and I will eat together at this table, taking it in turns to cook. I shall eventually retain one servant only, to wait at table when we have guests, and to help us teach the children.'

'The prostitutes' children?' asked Miss Curtis scornfully. 'Where do you imagine you are going to find staff to replace us with?'

'I've already found two people in the mountains. They don't like city life, so are willing to transform it.'

'What are you going to teach the children?' Miss Curtis demanded.

'It will depend on the size of the class, but the basic things, I thought: religion in a simple form, hygiene, and to read, write, count and think.'

'Are you a trained teacher?' Mr Baines inquired with raised eyebrows.

The goatee chuckled.

'Charlemagne was illiterate,' I answered, 'yet under him Alcuin was able to reform the handwriting of Europe. I shall train, as time permits.'

*

All week I felt peculiarly arid. But when the accounts had been scrutinised, and the household transferred; when I had bought some hens and goats, so that the servants need no longer bring eggs and milk daily; when the new building had been scrubbed, and I had made it clear that we all shared the responsibility for seeing that the floors were swept and mopped and sprayed every day to keep the insects down; when the garden had been dug, hoed, pruned and tidied, I felt better. There were already green figs, and a few coffee-trees; it would be a good idea to plant an apple orchard, and if we had our own hive we could afford with the money saved to grow some more flowers, both in the garden and the *patio* round which the house was planned.

There were not many flowers in Zone 5. I wanted ours to be visible through the open door, so that there was an immediate impression of leaves, cool, delicious, against a splash of brilliant blossom, an invitation to the quiet and shade that are not very far apart from holiness. Perhaps we could have a fountain too, if it was small: pure golden light and ceaselessly falling water, a central radiance at the end of long corridors secluded against the heat.

In the meantime I found a confessor, and made friends with some of the priests. Good sense, I learned, had been used with regard to the existing Indian religious beliefs. Much had politely to be ignored. Coatlicue—Our Lady of the Serpent Skirt—is associated with destruction and death as well as creation. She may be portrayed with a necklace of hands and hearts, her pendant a skull, claws her hands and feet. But she is also shown as a mother carrying her child. Concentration on her milder functions purified her cult. Similarly we condoned worship of the almond-eyed Virgin of Guadelupe; when we found anyone offering maize and beans to the Christ we were glad the offering was to Him instead of to Xipe the Flayed One; and if we found anyone offering maize and beans to Xipe, we dwelt on Xipe's resemblance to the Christ.

A greater orthodoxy could be imparted to the children of our prostitutes, since they were unaccustomed to any religious observances. Most of the prostitutes themselves thought our efforts funny. A few did not think them funny, but they giggled nevertheless. We waited. Three eventually came, furtive, shy, to us, and asked with a touch of defiance if we would still take their children's names. I explained that the list would never be closed.

Now the three had come, others would follow. There would be rebellions. There would be betrayals. Some of the renegades might in the end prove the most loyal. Then the prostitutes, or some of them, would ask if they too could be taught to read; and several would come to live with us. Most would return, unable themselves to live without money and men, but less inclined, now, to laugh at those who found they could. And there would be trouble with the owners of the brothels: men would come at night, belted, liquored up, with their minds on rape, bringing guns and fire and abuse. We should be given the strength to cope with all these situations.

The life was a desert of disappointment that we had taught ourselves to expect. Like other deserts, it had its own magnificence, and a few oases, which sometimes turned out to be mirage. One of the women, after living with us for a year, went back to her home village and married her child-hood sweetheart; *Deo volente*, her children will be brought up in the Catholic faith. Another, in whom we put high hopes, disappeared at night, taking with her a hundred dollars out of a fund of ours, and when next heard of had added one brothel more to those we had to deal with. Months passed, and we received a parcel containing one hundred and ten dollars. We sent back to her the equivalent in honey and dairy produce of the extra ten, explained that we charged no interest on our loans, and reminded her at the same time that she should have mentioned she was borrowing the money. We invited her to come and eat *gallo en chicha* with us the following Saturday, a departure from our usual diet. Being a woman of considerable courage, she came; and she stayed a whole week with us, before she went back.

2

The work was arduous, so I thought it sensible to try to see something of the pleasanter districts of Guatemala every day. The second zone appealed to me most. It was less frantic and newfangled than the fashionable parts, less shoddy, with less of tinsel and of trash. Bright yellow wooden dust-carts, drawn by hand, bumped along the muddy lanes; mule wagons rattled along the highways; the markets smelled of tamarind, garlic, sweet basil, parsley. Below the church baroque on the hill, a patch of waste land supplied grazing to the goats and donkeys, besides somewhere for the builders to store adobe bricks. It was still the capital, but it was a village.

Like the imperious vagrant I often saw there, his hat crammed down on long draggling locks, his beard as defiant as the holes in his jacket, I delighted especially in a little park:

JARDÍN DE ISABELLA CATÓLICA

where the students used to bring their lecture-notes and

inattentively forsake them, a few lovers met, and the children came to play.

> '*Vaya la papaya*
> *la vieja se desmaya*,'

they sang in the sun, open flies to their trousers, bare feet happy as they scuffed at the earth, brown fingers dabbling through the goldfish pond.

There was a fountain, a tiny one, there in the middle of the garden, keeping me reminded that the patio was still waterless. The charge for installation had proved to be more than we could reasonably spare, but I wondered from time to time if we could still somehow make one ourselves. The rains had brought relief to all parts of Guatemala, but not to me. Everyone who has engaged in evangelistic or social work of any kind must have met those scaly periods when the wells and springs of charity within dry up and need replenishment.

'You're tired, Celia,' they said at the mission. 'Shouldn't you take a week-end somewhere out of the city?'

'Oh, I don't like shirking,' I replied. 'This will pass if I don't give in to it. We can't afford yet the luxury of holidays!'

'Seriously, Celia, you ought to go, for everyone's sake,' my confessor remarked one day. 'If you think you're indispensable, you're beginning to fall into the danger of spiritual pride.'

In the end his warnings prevailed, and I took the bus for Antigua. Having neglected to pack lunch, I bought a *taco* and a cob of corn outside a church closed for restoration, and ate as I strolled through the town. A religious festival was in progress there : lemon streamers, white streamers, curved over the streets, the houses were decorated with lemon-and-white flags, all the children were on holiday.

Vendors of dolls, vendors of terracotta vases, vendors of chicle followed me. In the square before the cathedral, a haggard old man edged up, wordlessly offering a thin silver coin worn smooth at the rim, probably a family heirloom. The boy accompanying him said without looking at me, 'It costs five dollars.' They were not beggars, and they had not stolen it. The coin must have been worth more. I didn't know what to do. I would have asked them to eat something with me, but what I had brought was finished, and no shops were near. Regretfully I shook my head. They turned away at once, as if in relief, not insisting.

Entering the cathedral, I descended towards the crypt, where the icons were kept. It was hot with the many candles, and so small that, of five people worshipping, two had to stand outside, on the lowest step. My obeisance made, I left with no delay, meaning to act as pawnbroker to the old man, learn his history and see what could be done to help him redeem his pledge; but he had gone. Dejected and empty, I came to another church, and peeped round the west door.

Inside, it was immaculately, beautifully clean, hung with the same lemon and white streamers that decked each street, and pugent with *copal*.

A mutter of orisons reached me. Two nuns passed, all smiles, their keys and black beads chinking and dancing. Before me, in the chancel, the censer swung once more. I felt a little faint and dizzy; the smoking *copal* was heady stuff, the church overpoweringly full of flowers. Candles and gold swam before my eyes. Again there was the familiar feeling deep inside : an awe, not altogether pleasurable, without which I should be lifeless, lost; a hunger and a thirst, without which I should perish.

Prayer distanced the world. The candles, the smoke; the flowers, the other people dotted over the church, became irrelevant and far away. A pool grew, into which I ought to plunge, but always at the last I was afraid, I drew back, and the pool blended into the mundane objects once more close at hand.

Empty still, sick at heart, I arose and, having made my genuflexion, quitted the church. The sky outside was sullen. I strayed around the precincts, through an archway, across a court, then under another arch.

And there it was, there was the wonderful garden, with the fountain of pouring water. The walls were the dustiest, gentlest pink. Silver and shining, the water streamed into the air, high, high, in a spray so fine, so shimmering, so luminous that the ecstatic heart soared up to catch it and went beyond and was lost, past the seeking. In the basin beneath the pool, the stones were green and gold with translucent lichen, and then red, as garnets and rubies if they were purer would be red, as blood, or wine with the light in it, as the most delicate roses, can be red, redder than the coward spirit's wish. Time stopped, there in the wonderful garden, and only the fountain flowed, till all around was reverberation, a steady compulsive drumming, my hair, my face, my dress, wet, soaking. The man I had always known seized my hands and pulled me after him and we ran, both of us ran, till we were out of the torrent, and under the dark archway came silence, with the first rhapsody over and the beginning of another.

Was it wrong, then? Was what we did wrong?

I remember most how happiness brimmed, overflowing; our voices and the fountain, rising and falling in the garden. What we said is long forgotten, but I shall never forget the fountain or, a month later, during the journey over nocturnal roads, my first sight of fire-flies, which for some reason I had always expected to resemble glow-worms, but which looked in reality like flying silver stars. I shall remember, too, the old boatman with the long, drooping, concave upper lip, his smile that flashed like noonday sunshine as he ferried us across the waters strange with mangrove roots at night; the torches brought to light our way from the river; the first glimpse of the dancers in the village moving slow and solemn and grotesque round the hut, with sand all about them, and the indefatigable marimba. I shall remember how the children gravely chanted, advancing and retreating like the waves, in the ritual of one of their games; I shall remember, all my life, how we both watched them, while the smell of cooking came from the *rancho*; Paul's whistling as he went down to swim, and how I stood by the two huts, looking into the darkness after him even when he had ceased to be visible, rather than turn, and make my choice.

The voices of the children were clearer suddenly, for the breeze had again dropped :

> *La rana no está aquí,*
> *Estará en su vergél,*
> *Cortando una rosa,*
> *Sembrando un clavel.'*

Shouts summoned them to bed.

And there came to my mind a picture of how, at the beginning of one of her more self-destructive affairs, Anne had approached my room in college, and said, standing in the doorway. 'Oh, Celia, Celia, you're *good*, but have you ever really been tempted?'

Then she said thickly, 'Tonight I slept with a man, I didn't know his name...'

Angry, because I loved her, I broke out, 'Anne, you're not a child! Your exhibitionism will wreck other people's lives, as well as your own!'

And her face went blank, and she very quietly closed the door, and went away. Only then did it occur to me that she had come not to make a boast, but to seek an explanation.

I went over to the window, but across the quad her room, if she had gone there, was already dark.

*

Shadows loomed and tangled on the sands, around the fires where flame and the night met. Moorish blood pulsing, the throaty guitar sobbed, the guitar plucked atavistic antique rhythms out of darkness. Men's voices had replaced those of the children. I turned, and entered Paul's hut.

Was it wrong, then? Was what we did wrong?

In nobody's eyes next morning could I see awareness that we were more evil now than we had been before. The colours of the *rancho* were as soft and as clean. When, after breakfast, we went down to talk with the ferryman, he smiled at us as before, and as before his smile was the sun striking the sea.

The sea gleamed and glittered, the sea danced, there was sea and sand in our eyes, on our lips, all over our faces as we made love. Light struck the coconut palms and they glittered too, gnarled like a tree the old man's face glittered, the writhing mangrove-roots were strange in the light of day as they had been the night we arrived. Criss-cross palm-leaves fanned the air, lifting into fronds so that the air itself became fronds that waved, green breaths of coolness out of the glitter and the sand and the sun.

Was it wrong, then, what we did? Was what we did wrong?

116

Marimba music came plangent over the sands at night. The children did not sing any more, they had gone away, gone home, but the young men sang, erotic and fierce and melancholy their songs. Was it wrong, then, what we did?

Was what we did wrong? The milk of the green coconuts had become effervescent, from fermenting in the sun. At noon, stunned by the glitter and strong light, I lay dizzily on the palm-mat in our *rancho*, listening to Paul read, watching the water dry slowly on his back. Was it about God that he was reading? Was what we did wrong?

When he dropped the book and went down to swim once more, I still lay listlessly on the palm-mat, its fibres poking stiffly into my back. The sand was grey. The shadow was black. White, the sunshine dazzled. To drink would mean going across the burning sands, and the coconut milk had fermented. My throat was parched. I lay on the palm-mat, with the stiff fibres poking into my back.

'Are you all right?'

He had returned to fetch his dark glasses and a towel.

I opened my eyes, but couldn't summon the will to reply.

'Celia, are you all right?' he asked again.

With an enormous effort I nodded. 'Sleepy, though.'

'Come and take a dip, it will freshen you up.'

'You go.'

'Sure?'

Satisfied, he strolled off towards the sea. I sat up. The sand in the hut was very strange, was dark grey. I stared at it. And black the shadow, white the sun.

Sunstroke, I thought suddenly. Sunstroke can be like epilepsy, with its flicker-fits. Avoid contrasts of light and dark. Avoid walking under tall coconut-palms that glitter green and make the shade harsh. Avoid . . .

Avoid? I thought. The grey and white and black are strange. A void . . .? Avoid . . .

On waking, I went limply down the shore, a long distance, away from all the *ranchos*, till I could walk no farther.

Was what we did wrong? I tried to think lying in the sand, and swimming in the sea I tried to think, but the sand was intense, the sea glittered, in this fusion of blue and gold to think was impossible.

Far out on the ocean white sails flashed. Tumbling waves and spray the sea flung crinkled kaleidoscopic coinage up, sucked argent its coinage back, tossed silver coinage rumbling with a lurch and scrunch and a crash on the beach.

The way back was so much longer than the way out. I paused, sandals in hand. A brown-bodied man was wading towards me. He was wet and glittering, and the light flashed from his eyes, from his skin; he said, 'You're not coming into the sea?'

I looked at him intently. He laughed, and stretched out his hand, and made a gesture towards the sea, a gesture of invitation; his eyes travelled over me, deliberately, brazenly, and he laughed again and gestured at the glittering wet sea.

'You're not going to swim?'

For a moment I thought of the two of us, the bronze brown-bodied man and me, lying in the sand together, and he saw what was in my mind, and his eyes were hot saying, 'Pretty gringa, gringa linda.' My eyes were on him, he was golden, drops of water ran glistening down his brown body into the sea.

Then I shook my head. He followed me, at a short distance, curiously. Once I looked back. He pointed again at the sea. I went on, till I came to the rancho, and to Paul.

Was it then I told him it was wrong? Everything has become muddled up. Sometimes I think it was then, sometimes I think I had already said it the day before. Perhaps I said it then.

Where was I standing when the man spoke to me? Surely I had been on the sand, not wading? Yet we were close, and the water ran in crooked glistening rivulets down his body, salt into the sea.

When did I say it was wrong? Did I say it was wrong? Was it wrong, then, what we did? Was what we did wrong?

I know Paul asked me if I was happy, and though I said 'Yes', it was the beginning of when I was not.

3

' "Remember that no man loses any other life than this which now he lives, nor lives any other than this which now he loses",' Paul read out, glancing up from his Marcus Aurelius. 'Isn't that exactly what I've been trying to tell you, darling? Here you are, sending me away to save me, and if we have no soul, I shan't even be able to say: "Yah, I told you so," and you'll never know what a dreadful waste your piety was!'

I said uncertainly, 'Being alive means taking risks; some are smaller than others. Perhaps the tragedy was a farce and we have no soul—but if a soul we have, sending yours to Hell is the most terrible of all the sins I could imagine or commit.'

'Celia!' he mocked. 'Since when have you gone in for gambling, or admitted the possibility that there may be no more soul in us than in the stuffing of this armchair? Am I converting you at last, my little one?'

'I think you are,' I said after a moment. 'And for that reason I must go from here.'

'Oh, you're not serious!'

I made no answer.

'You *can't* mean it,' he said angrily. 'You're too intelligent for that! Let's talk it over.'

'There's nothing to talk over, Paul. You're married. I was engaged in mission work. Your wife is one of my friends. The issues are quite clear.'

'Celia, you don't believe this nonsense any more,' he said, his tone strong and firm. 'At some time or other every child has to learn to stop sucking its thumb. It's absurd for you to give up happiness from a whim you've really outgrown, an outworn fantasy, a caprice of conscience!'

I pressed my hands tiredly to my eyes, which ached from sleeplessness. 'I can no longer attend Mass. I'm closing the mission centre. But that makes no difference to the situation between you and me.'

His laugh was short, incredulous, but suddenly he saw, as I had seen, that discussion would solve nothing, and all his confidence left him. 'Need you close the mission, if . . .?'

'I can no longer attend Mass,' I repeated.

The room had become as sad as a railway station late at night, set in limbo, with a wail of passing trains.

'When will you go?' Paul asked.

'At the end of this week, or early the next.'

He said suddenly, 'Were you lonely in this room, Celia?'

'A little,' I responded.

He cried, 'You had your faith!'

I hoped he would not kiss me, and he did not kiss me. We did not touch each other, we did not say goodbye, we did not say anything more. When at last, quietly, he had gone, as people go into the train across the other platform, the whole room seemed to depend from my body. The walls were stretched tight, like a bubble. If I had swallowed, or let a hot gush of tears escape from my eyes, it would all have disintegrated.

Everyone at the mission understood, when I haltingly explained to them I was leaving. I think they had known, from the first day in Antigua, all that would happen.

'Will you carry on without me?' I asked.

'No,' they replied. 'We will wait for you to come back.'

'And if I don't come back?'

*

My prostitutes had not known.

'But why are you going, why?' they insisted.

A story had been prepared, for me to tell them. I could not utter it. 'I met a man . . .' I faltered.

'Ah,' they said softly, 'a man!' and for a while they asked nothing more.

One of them wondered, 'But if he was a good man . . .?'

The youngest spat. 'A good man!' she jeered.

'He was married. He was good in his way, but not a believer.'

'Ah,' they said softly, 'a married man!'

'They're the worst, they're the worst, the married ones! That Paco Jiménez, the other day, you know what he wanted me to do?'

'Ssh!'

'Well, don't we all have bodies?' said the youngest, with a laugh, then fell silent, slinking furtive glances at me.

'*La carne. Sí, pues.*'

'*Tan triste, la vida. Triste, triste, triste.*'

'And our children?' asked one. 'Their lessons?'

They all turned round and harshly shushed her. 'How could you think that the *señora* was going to spend her life here with us, her so pretty, with the white skin, the fine manners, and us what we are?'

'I was going to spend my life here,' I said. 'My whole life I was going to spend here.'

'But now you will go back to your country,' they comforted me, 'and you will be happy there.' They sighed. '*Ay, tan triste la vida. Triste, triste, triste.*'

*

I did not know what to do while waiting to leave. The thought of once more travelling to Antigua treacherously entered my mind, but I thrust it away. The thought of once more, for the last time, travelling to Antigua Guatemala entered my mind. I thrust it away. The thought of once more . . .

Only the last rains had still to fall, and theoretically it would be the cool season again. It was hotter than ever in the city. The air was so bright that almost all colour had been blenched, except from the glittering azure and purple mountains. The pavements looked like white silk, and the churches, the houses, the shops threw on them an unsought darkness that gave only the illusion of shade. Water poured in steep parabolas of silver from the fountain in the Parque Central, but to cross to it would have meant moving through urban traffic-filled deserts in the sun's sheerest intensity, to be withered to whiteness, like the flowers, and the wilting grass.

The tiny fountain at the Jardín de Isabella Católica in Zone 2 lacked significance, was not worth the visit or the long journey, contained only children, students, vagabonds.

In Antigua, the volcano called Fuego, fire, was in eruption. Never go back. Never revisit the place where you discovered the fountain and the garden, the cuckoo's song, the rainbow, the pot of shining gold.

At the same hour as before I took the bus to Antigua. Acatenango, Agua, were not in eruption, and Fuego lay quiescent, not as though its wrath was burned out, but as though it had never flung incendiary bombs raging heavenwards, to kill seven people as they tended their fields of maize. Sleepy, the town mused and slumbered, beggar-filled, buzzing with flies, as it had been for hundreds of years.

No one was in the cathedral. No one was in its square. The crypt, hot with candles, was empty.

There were no lemon and white streamers in the streets or in the church. There were no flags. There were no lemon and white flowers. No nuns passed with black beads dancing, no keys jingled, no one smiled.

The court with the fountain had changed its position, and it had shrunk. How dusty the walls were, dusty the pillars, dusty the arches and the brass-studded door! Meaninglessly water flowed through air and fell back into water, water fell into water in the dusty basin and made mud.

Men's minds work differently from those of women. I waited there for Paul all day by the hot pink shrunken walls. Never go back to where you discovered the fountain and the garden, the cuckoo's song, the rainbow, the pot of shining gold. I waited there for Paul all day, watching spiders scuttle over debris, watching spiders scuttle through the dust. Never, never, never go back.

*

It was night when I reached El Cerrito, in the second zone. On the hillside were bonfires where women patted maize into *tortillas* to make *tacos*, and scorched flakes of charcoal, orange, scarlet, black, with the ancient unforgettable smell of blue pine-smoke, flew showering in sparks up into the darkness.

I had intended to walk anywhere where silence was: in the little garden, perhaps, now glow-worms pricked red holes in the grass and flames burned on the hillside; but on hearing the din of loudspeakers, marimbas, shouts and laughter, I began to drift like a ghost towards their social noise. I stood a while watching, by the lake that mirrored the whirling wavering lights of the wheel and dipper, in my nostrils the smell of cinnamon, limes, frying bacon, burning wood, cigars. Suddenly I made my way down into the fair and bought *enchiladas*, the chilli catching in my throat, piquant, the sauce dribbling thick down my fingers. Always fairs had fascinated me: the desolation, the loneliness at their core.

People jostled about the booths where trinkets caught the light: logies, paste jewels. Rifle-ranges imitated the poppings of champagne corks, and like breaking bubbles the frothy incandescent laughter faded again. Tattered canvas let through starlight in pin-points. Rearing and heaving horses, snarling tigers, lolloping harmless lions were gay and at the same time unbearably sad, touched up here and there with new paint that drew attention to the loose festering scabs of the old. Flaring pink torches of spun candy-floss, their holders unseen, bobbed mysteriously through the night—'like chiffon scarves,' Anne had once said, canvas jammed against her hip, quickly painting, 'cheap, gaudy, forgivable.'

Watching, I was transported away into the years of child-hood, was listening intently again to tales told by ravenous grown-ups: of lollipops and liquorice; caramels, comfits, mouth-watering, tongue-melting, lavishly honeyed sweets; transparent cubes that, shaken, made snow fall on the houses imprisoned within; apples dipped in toffee; bull's-eyes, sticky and striped; lemonade powder; pig money-boxes; mice of glistening white sugar—all the things we were too old to delight in when the war was over, and, shut out of the Pied Piper's cave, could not have while it was on; for whose loss (conscious only in the more imaginative, merely causing the delinquency of the rest) our parents were no more accountable to us, I once had argued with Anne, than Adam had been to them for losing Eden.

*

'They themselves think they're guilty!' Anne had cried, wedging the more firmly her canvas. 'Only to us they won't admit it! All the "We can't understand what they're angry about" stuff, when they must know, damned well! And "Why are they so apathetic to politics?" when in the name of politics one part of the world bundled its opposition into Buchenwald, and the others, our parents, who were on the "right" side, not only condoned the stringing-up of Mussolini's dead body by a baying mob, but also used the entire civilian population of two cities as guinea-pigs for research into leukaemia! *They* may claim Hiroshima was somehow more excusable than Belsen, but I wouldn't dare! At Sodom and Gomorrah even barbarous old Jahveh is supposed to have waited to hear if there were ten righteous men!'

'Anne, in war people can't think clearly!'

'Try telling the Yanks that! According to them, everybody can sit down and play it like nuclear chess!'

'Anne . . .'

'Of course people can't think in war! But why did the war ever start, who made them go banging their heads against the wall? Why did they ignore what Churchill *repeatedly* told them? Why did they continue to disarm while Germany and Japan were arming? Would you call what that generation did *before* the war, "thinking"?'

'Everyone can make rather horrifying mistakes,' I said.

'They made a sight too many; we paid. And now we're to sit down and take advice from them, just because they're older? We're to be grateful to them, just because so many of them got in the way of a bullet or came back with artificial limbs? Well, I suppose we should be, we should be grateful they chose to drop their bombs on the Japanese and not on us. Sometimes I wake up at night shivering with gratitude, I'm so grateful I don't get back to sleep.'

'Can't you try to put yourself in their place?'

'I can try, but I hope to God I never succeed. The nearest I can reach is realising what a small price the childhood of a generation must have seemed to them for the sport, the frolic, the team spirit, of war.'

'But consider the position they were in, Anne! Czechoslovakia . . .'

'Czechoslovakia! That's rich! What has this country ever cared about the Czechs? Or the Poles? The Jews? Haven't you ever taken a look at the housing adverts?' Scrubbing a smudge off the painting, she laughed. 'Why should I get so worked up about it, anyway? *They* never do.'

'I must confess I don't understand why you react so violently. It's over. You'd do better to help other people—do some famine relief work, for instance—than wallow in self-pity.'

'*Self*-pity?' Anne said incredulously. 'It's not *me* I pity; it's not *pity* I feel. I just boil with rage at the thought of all the inarticulate ones, smashing windows and being asked by pious old magistrates, "What did you do it for, my boy?" Christ! It's not that they smash windows that's surprising, but that they ever stop! "Over"—what do you mean, "it's over"? It's hardly started. Our most discerning philosopher's got a bigger following now than he had before the *last* war! As for me, before you ask me to make any "constructive suggestions" I'm going off to get bloody drunk, so toddle home, love, go have yourself an orgy of old clothes and cast-off jewellery! When the British War of Independence comes to your notice, remember I told you, but don't invite me to participate; I've been fighting it all my life!'

*

'Celia?'

I started.

'You're really leaving?' asked my confessor, from the hilltop.

'Next week.'

'You could still suffer God to change your mind.'

'If there's a God,' Anne had said, 'He should have been in

the dock at the war trials, He should be in the dock the whole time. . . . But belief in Him is only the sanctification of the tenet that the end justifies the means.'

'Search for the scapegoat!' I had murmured.

'I beg your pardon?'

'Did I speak? I'm sorry. I was thinking aloud.'

'You would do better to pray.'

'Does one exclude the other?' I asked.

'In your case, my daughter!'

We both glanced back at the fair as we descended towards the bus-stop. A young man in a swing-boat called something out to a girl every time he passed her, and she, in her own swing-boat, strained forward every time to catch what he was saying, but every time failed, shaking her head. Showman's supercilious mustachios drooping, an older man tore into fragments a heap of tickets, acid pink, electric blue, letting them float from his finger-ends against the night and be borne, confetti, away on the breeze.

My confessor took my hands. '*Vaya con Dios.*'

'With God? I've no faith left.'

Over the dark sky a last few fireworks whizzed, flared and sputtered.

'Take mine, and go with Him.'

4

England was a foreign country.

Used to the sight of begging-bowls, I had forgotten that in London poverty wasn't a misfortune, to be broadcast on the heights and in the depths, but, since officially the need for it had ceased to exist, a peculiarly disreputable crime, whose authorship no one wished to discover. The part of life I had shunned in Guatemala was here inescapable: the affluent society oozed, reeking, all around me, inviting me, on its expense accounts, out to lunch, where it chatted with unctuous enthusiasm about the hypocrisy of the Victorians. Having no head for initials, no Sprachgefühl for bureaucrats, in the Civil Service I felt an unredeemable foreigner, dubious of the drainage, expatriate in my own land.

What, I kept demanding, is *wrong* with me? It was as if all my life I had been led blindfold, rejoicing in the unseen sun, and then, in a strange country, the smothering bandages around my head were snatched off, I was shown mountains, valleys, rivers, seas—and whisked away, even while, shielding my brow against the blaze of light, I became conscious, amid the black, of gold.

A man once blind regards the squat dark telephone and doubtfully measures it against its shrill cry. A parachutist dropped into an unfamiliar, charted territory acknowledges its agreement with his data, but can accept its name only by an act of faith. I looked at memory's illusive photographs; glancing through the album I remembered this hint of laughter, that effect of light, but could no longer recall with what meaning they must once have been endowed. Curious phantom, haunting the house of yesterday. I turned up old diaries, notebooks, a letter to Janice that had never been sent :

' . . . it was awfully difficult to make anyone see that I haven't *decided* to go to Guatemala. If a decision was involved, it wasn't mine, so there won't be any afterthoughts or wonderings.'

None had been written to replace the unposted letter; secure in my halo I had disappeared abroad with no goodbyes, and not corresponded with Janice since. What communication could I have with her now, in the memory of what had passed between her husband and me?

Between her husband and me . . .

*

In a moment it was the party again, and Roddy and I, through the hubbub of voices, the dazzle of bright lights after darkness, were searching for our host. Across the room I caught sight of him suddenly, and next to him, as always, Anne.

Whenever she found herself in the middle of a polite conversation with strangers (there were so many people she wished to remain strange) a desperate look crossed her face, as though, outside, a saddled horse was waiting for her, and she had only to go through the doors to reach it; but to do that was impossible, because she was tied invisibly to Paul, and he would not move.

As if operating a camera I watched her, noting her smile in almost the right places, nod, look incredulous or consoling, now and then interpose a remark of her own, all with the same repressed impatience, the air of belonging elsewhere, far away, outside. Paul, at her elbow, asked her something, and she took, with an inquiring glance, the glass of one of the strangers and handed it over, with her own. Having, in that moment, become aware of our presence, she excused herself to her other guests and hastened over, giving rapid instructions to the barman *en route*.

' 'Lo, both of you, I thought you were never coming! Roddy, go and announce yourself to Paul, he'll be glad of the chance to escape. Here, have a noggin, Celie love. Pretty dress —the stole's Mexican? Honest to God, these people drive one to drink!' She tossed off the brandy in her glass as illustration. 'How are you?'

'Soberer than you!'

'I'm not tight, worse luck, only melancholy. All parties have this effect on me, 'specially ours. Nothing to do with the drinks —though I wouldn't touch the punch if I were you, I think Paul must have misread the labels.'

'What's that about misreading the labels?' he asked.

'Oh, there you are!' She looked round. 'You *haven't* left poor Roddy with the Blight? Honestly, Paul!' She advanced to the rescue, but Roddy was already extricating himself, and she swerved abruptly towards another group, whose monopoly of the crisps and olives she seemed, with a tolerance unusual in her, to approve.

'Have some punch?' Paul asked.

I laughed. 'Thanks awfully, I'm happy with this. You're keeping well?'

He nodded absently. 'How's the Min. of Ed. these days?'

And across these vacancies with which we filled silence, 'Don't you remember, don't you remember?' I was asking, and 'Why should I remember, what's the use?' said his noncommittal stare.

At the other side of the room, puffing a strand of hair out of her eyes and rolling them in elaborate dumb-show, Anne drew a finger slowly across her throat and mimed imminent collapse. About to say, 'I think Anne wants you', I felt, for the first time, a terrible pang of jealousy. I looked up at him, and for a moment, though he had not budged, we both thought he was going to kiss me. Spasmodically he put his left hand against the wall before him, so that I was enclosed.

His hand dropped again. 'Sorry, lost my balance! You look rather pale, what's the matter?'

'I swallowed too much of this concoction in one go,' I lied, holding up my glass.

He bent and sniffed. 'Smells lethal,' he said, surprised. 'Much better have some punch?'

'No, really, thanks. Anne's trying to catch your attention, look!'

She said something to him, and they drew apart from the others. In the opposite corner to mine, apparently thinking herself unobserved, she raised her mouth, and, absorbed, clasped in a still violence, they kissed. He looked about, not in my direction, and nodded towards the stairs. She hesitated, then I read the word 'Later' on her lips. Shaken, as always, at such glimpses of other people's private lives, I turned away, and saw Roddy also watching them. To my mind, in confused snatches, came episodes from a recurring dream of the four of us; but now the situation was reversed, for in that dream Anne and Paul watched from different parts of a room while Roddy and I engaged in the preliminaries of love.

The liquid in my glass was quivering; I drank it angrily down. When next I lifted my eyes, Anne was again before me. I suddenly wondered if she had known she was observed, but her face showed only the withdrawn, intent look I had seen on it many times of old.

'How's the melancholy?' I asked.

'I really think it's religious in origin,' Anne responded. 'It always comes over me when I'm doing something I enjoy.'

'While you're doing it?' I forced myself to say. 'Dear, dear!'

She laughed. 'Afterwards. Or sometimes before.'

'It happens with everything you enjoy?'

'Yes; but then I only enjoy things I've been told are wrong.'

'Does the converse work?' I asked.

'What—if you told me that it was sinful to go to church, would I like going? I don't think it's as simple as that, but the ordinary conditioning has gone on too long now for me to be able to tell. You know, you've changed!' she said. 'Once you reminded me of a saint, but you don't so much now. It takes all the pleasure out of baiting you.'

'I'm sorry.'

'Is the room spinning, Celia, or is it me?'

'You, I think.'

'In that case I'll stay and talk to you till I'm sober, if you don't mind,' she said. 'I hate drunken hostesses, don't you, they're an incitement to general licence. You didn't remind me of just *any* saint,' she recapitulated, 'but my favourite ones : St Joan, for example.'

'But you used to think she was unhinged! '

'I still do. That's probably where the appeal lies—though not the resemblance to you! Don't *you* think she was a bit touched?'

'She doesn't seem to have shown any signs of abnormality apart from her visions and her voices.'

'*Apart* from her visions and her voices! But really, is it any saner to think you talk with St Michael and All Angels than to think you are yourself one of them? And what possible faith can you have in voices that told her she'd win her breach-of-promise suit?'

'She did win it, didn't she?'

'Oh, Celia! Listen, if ever the Archangel Gabriel comes down to remind me to post my coupon for the football pools . . .'

'We'll call a doctor. Yes. I see what you mean.'

There was an awkward pause; she gave a little smile, and I hurried on, 'It's hardly in the best traditions of unworldliness. But don't you regard it as a miracle that St Joan could face the fire of which she was so much afraid?'

'Not to be nasty, but she probably believed the flames down below lasted longer! No, I withdraw that—unfair! I wouldn't deny she was brave. But didn't Edith Cavell or one of those other tiresome women, Nightingale or Darling, say "Patriotism is not enough"? If you're going to canonise Joan of Arc merely for dying an heroic death, won't you have to do the same for Clara Petacci, Mussolini's mistress? She could have done a bunk rather than end still trying to save him, with a rattle of bullets against a shed.'

I gave an exclamation of disgust.

'Or,' she said, eyes glinting, 'aren't we far enough away from the last war to be as objective in our judgements about that as about the Hundred Years War? Saint or no saint, the little French peasant didn't seem on the right side when we burned her at Rouen!'

'You admire some very strange people!' I said.

'I don't know anything about Clara Petacci except the way she died, and what happened to her body afterwards at the hands of the gallant Italian partisans. If you're going to tell me about atrocities she condoned, it won't alter my respect for her courage, any more than thinking she was loony affects my opinion of St Joan's willingness to go into the fire rather than recant again. Besides, little Joan's charming ambivalence towards men entertains me: one minute stripping in front of the soldier lads, the next donning armour to keep them at bay! Still, she hardly went as far as that other female saint, who grew a beard in the interests of her chastity. . . .'

'Liberata, you mean? The apocryphal one?'

'I prefer her other name,' said Anne. 'Uncumber. And I like to believe in her.'

Paul caught her eye, and after going through the motions of searching for a handkerchief, with a mutter she slipped towards the stairs.

Signalling at Roddy, who acquiesced, I adjusted my stole.

'My regards to Anne, and thank you both for a lovely evening,' I said. 'We're just going.'

'It was nice seeing you here, even so briefly,' Paul responded. Whether the expression in his eyes was for me or for Anne I do not think he himself knew, but when I waited on the landing for Roddy to collect his coat, the staircase was already empty, and in all the mirrors we saw them again embraced.

5

Blown on the black wind, in the Circle of the Lustful, amid the Sins of the Leopard,

> *'Nessun maggior dolore*
> *Che ricordarsi del tempo felice*
> *Nella miseria',*

Paolo's mistress told Dante and his Mantuan guide. To recall happiness in misery is, it is true, a spiteful sorrow; yet unless such misery and such sorrow came, we should never bethink ourselves of the happy time, contrive for it no shape, nor experience its fullest form and subtlety. The time of sadness one can thankfully dwell on in better or in worse days; the happy time is recollected only in worse.

'Roddy knows neither hell nor heaven!' Anne once cried. Desperate in her consciousness of both, she forgot that either can be visited and not recognised. Unaware of it I had entered heaven; aware, I was entering hell. In a parched desert or jeered at by monkeys in a fever-ridden jungle I journeyed, seeking again the land of innocence.

So often I had instructed others how to find the way back. 'You believed once,' I had said to Janice. 'Hold fast to your ball of twine, and you'll come, still living, from your labyrinth.'

'And if the twine is broken?' she asked. 'If the corridors are made of sand?'

'Then look for the sun, direct yourself by that!'

'The sun is in eclipse. Don't tell me to pray, Celia, or I shall slap you. I *have* prayed; the whole of my work is prayer. Ah, you make me earnest, you make me irritable, and I don't like that!'

'Work on,' I said. 'You know very well the twine isn't broken.'

She answered, 'Life would be so much easier if it was! One would have a whole desert to die in, instead of this pathetic little foot-marked strip of dust.'

*

Other encounters there had been: conversations with Anne, with Paul, with Roderick—with Stephen, before he died. The strangest of them all had taken place when I was slumming in Islington, years ago.

The snow, which, the previous day, had melted to brown slush, froze during the night. Early next morning more fell. People walked with an absurd caution that did not prevent a leg from treacherously skidding under them so that they swooped and plunged, scrabbling for their dignity, and regained their balance with a sense of disaster-only-just-escaped, a rapidly thudding heart. At night it snowed again, in tufts floating aimless on an icy sky.

I had to go out to telephone Roddy. The snow was already thick, squeaking and crunching underfoot. I was pushing the last coin into the slot when a tap sounded on the glass door, and a girl with flushed cheeks and soft, pretty, loose hair diamonded with melting snow asked me if she could make an emergency call.

Remarking, 'Don't put any more money in', I came out and waited on the bleak and freezing corner. When I looked back to see if she had nearly finished, the girl was not speaking; her attitude suggested that she was checking something, and as I gazed she lifted and turned her wrist, with a downward glance.

When she pushed the door open I asked, 'You didn't get your number?'

'No—no,' she said absently.

For a moment I wondered, from her air of excitement and exaltation, if she was deranged. Whatever the situation was, I felt some responsibility for her.

'It's my husband,' she said suddenly. 'I overheard a conversation—tonight he's taking somebody else to a cinema near here, but I don't know which. I wanted to find out.'

Unconvinced by her tale, I still felt, realising that she might have been asking the times of performance, faintly ashamed of my disbelief.

'Wouldn't it be better to go home now and have it out with him tomorrow?'

She shook her head, with a curious little giggle.

'What's the film called?'

'I don't even know that,' she said, giggling again. 'Only that the word "snow" occurs in the title.'

'*The Snows of Kilimanjaro* is on at the place round the corner.'

From the direction in which she had come it was probable she had passed the cinema and seen the title herself.

'That could be it,' she responded.

'Do you want to go there?'

'You don't think it would be wise?'

'Come and have some coffee while we discuss it. My flat's just along the road.'

As she went with me to the house and followed me up the stairs to the top floor I wondered what she could be playing at. Her story had every appearance of having been trumped up at a moment's notice, nothing about it had any plausibility, and I did not know in the least what to make of her. Her voice, speech and manner were those of the self-educated, but the direct style in which she had come to the point, her offhand acceptance of my invitation and of the coins left in the telephone booth, belonged to entirely another class: the moneyed loafers of Chelsea and Kensington.

Coffee was set before her.

'Well, Miss Farmer, why did you choose Guatemala for your mission?' she asked. 'Aren't there enough slums for you in Islington?'

I stared.

'Jasmine Donald's the name,' she said coolly. 'I was going to gate-crash, but seeing you there on the corner was too good a chance to miss.'

'You would have been perfectly welcome had you rung at the door in the usual way. I should have much preferred it to the story you've spun.'

'Oh, on one plane the story was true!' she replied, amusedly treating my anger as an irrelevance.

'What is it you want?' I asked.

'My paper's short of news, for one thing. "MISSIONARY QUITS MISSION", you know? For another, I'd like to further my education, to find my way to, if you like, God. Though' (the amusement still lurked in her eyes) 'it's always very nice just to talk to people with posh accents like yours.'

'I'm afraid I'm too busy to receive reporters or purely social visits,' I said. 'If you're serious about wishing to have some religious guidance I can put you in touch with someone who will help you.'

'You're asking me to leave, in other words? And we have so much in common, too!'

I hesitated, but declined to take the bait. 'This woman your husband is with ...?' I inquired.

'I didn't say anything about a woman.'

'But I thought ...'

'It's a man,' she said. 'Though actually I don't have a husband.'

There was something conspiratorial in the atmosphere. I suddenly realised that I intensely disliked being alone with her; disliked and feared our physical proximity.

Abruptly I arose. 'I'm sorry about your allegorical plight, but, as I say, I'm busy, and now I have to telephone my brother.'

'You'll find he's gone to the cinema,' she said.

'I think not! He's expecting my call!'

She shrugged, finished her coffee, and stood up.

'Why are you afraid of me?' she asked. She giggled again. 'Are you that way as well?'

'This conversation is ridiculous, and I don't wish to continue it. I really don't think there's anything further I can do for you,' I said stiffly.

'There's a good deal you could have done, but if you don't want to do so, it's your own concern, of course.'

'Are you *threat*ening me?' I asked.

'I never make threats,' she said pleasantly, her eyes unsmiling.

We went downstairs and trudged without more speech to the end of the white road, where I pointed out the station. Glancing back, I saw her cross towards the cinema where *The Snows of Kilimanjaro* was showing. She waved to me with complete self-possession before engaging in conversation with the girl at the ticket window.

When I rang Roddy's flat, there was no reply. He had gone to see a film, with a friend of his from Winchester.

*

Once, in our student days, on the way to a lecture, I came upon Anne watching some children.

'Why are they laughing like that, Celia?' she said. 'None of them has said anything funny.'

I looked at them. 'They're laughing because they're happy,' I said.

She was astonished, then amused. 'Is that why babies laugh?' she asked, liking the idea. Then, gradually, her brow furrowed, and she said, 'But I don't think, for these children, it's right. They're older, they're not irresponsible any more. Happiness shouldn't be so *unaware*!'

'Oh, Anne!' I exclaimed.

'But don't you see,' she said vehemently, 'they'll never *know* they were happy!'

It was on the tip of my tongue to say, 'And you, who would know if you were happy, will never be!' But I saw the same thought occur to her, and felt regret.

'We recognise their happiness, so it won't have been a waste.'

'Is that the royal "we", or am I included out of politeness?'

We had reached Schools, but she seemed about to go past. 'Haven't you a lecture?' I asked, stopping.

'Probably, yes.'

'Aren't you going to it?'

'What for?' she said.

'Because, for one thing, you'll be sent down if you don't at least look as though you're working.'

'Appearances!' she said indifferently. 'Any work I did at the moment would be awful.' She mimicked: ' "Write me a good essay, Miss Rivers, or you'll lose your scholarship." "Anne, pull yourself together, or you'll go down." Can you imagine anything less likely to produce the desired result? Most of them take literally Johnson's dictum that when a man knows he's to be hanged in a fortnight, it wonderfully concentrates his mind.'

'You know your attitude-striking worries them, Anne. You don't give them a chance.'

'Do you suppose my attitude-striking doesn't worry me? In the men's colleges if anyone's muddled up they let him sort himself out on his own. But women always get involved, always start breathing down one's neck.'

'If they didn't watch you . . .'

'I'd have more chance of reverting to normal,' she said quietly. Then the jeers began again. ' "Think about the rest of the community. Think about Society. Be objective. Don't you care about anything except yourself?" But I can't say "I care" without laughing, and I don't feel like embroidering it on my Gown.'

'You hate this place?' I asked.

The red flamed in her cheeks as hotly as if she had been slapped. 'I admire their brains so much that I can forgive them their ruthlessness to people only by remembering it's one I share. I love this place. It's neither my fault nor theirs that we don't speak the same language just now. Who'd have forecast that I'd turn into a Romantic, in a Classical age? But look—you'll be late!'

'You really won't come?'

'I shall do the other thing they're always advising, and go

for a stroll. Splendid cure for introspection, fresh air! Fresh air, and plenty of milk.' She wilted visibly. 'Vitamin deficiency is their latest. No one can say they don't try! The only permanent solution is euthanasia, but I'll have to wait till *they* suggest it, or they'll think I'm being sarcastic again.'

*

The arid sands that had enclosed and isolated her so many times were all around me now. Eternity itself was mirage, oases were hallucination. The very desert I sought to cross might not exist, but I believed in it, and it seemed to have no end. The valley I travelled, the dry valley, led back to birth. Before birth was nothingness. It led forward to death, after which was probably nothingness again.

Focus on that nothingness, a voice inside me said, and you will survive. But nothingness cannot be limited. It seems not negative, but all too positive, too comprehensive, in its abstraction. The millions of stars that circle the blue night are not nothingness, their sum is infinite, yet in contemplating them the mind reels.

Forms lacking substance, people drifted in patterns that were as purposeless, as devoid of meaning, as transitory, as the pieces of coloured tinsel scattered in a child's toy, or as shifting light on waves blown by the soft breezes of summer. I drifted also, shaken in a puzzle, flotsam on a plunging sea.

Yet suddenly, with no responsibility of mine, I might in time's full course be cast up, gaping, on a warm stretch of coast; might flounder in the last inches of retreating water, and, flecked with foam, stumble, exhausted, to my knees upon the strand; might dash the wet hair back from my face, and, with my eyes screwed up against the flow of light, might, weary in every limb, content with comprehending nothing, move, once more, haltingly, towards it :

'*L'amor che move il sole e l'altre stelle*'

—the Love which moves the sun and every other star.

Duologue four

Conciliatorily, 'How did your lecture go?' Anne asked when next Paul made an appearance. 'Shame that you're so often taken away from your book!'

It was the wrong approach. 'My book!' he said glumly, and sagged over the chair-back, staring again at the manuscript-cluttered table.

Catching sight of her perturbed face, he straightened up, the movement rocking the chair against him so that its front legs left the ground. 'Oh, the lecture was all right!' He released the chair. 'It was on mind and personality; I wandered a bit into psychology, perhaps, but no harm done: introverts, extraverts, that sort of thing.'

'Extraverts don't exist,' said she.

'And how do you make that one out?' he asked.

'You remember Descartes: "I think, therefore I am"? Well . . .'

'His conclusion didn't logically follow. "I think, therefore thought is." '

'Yes, I've seen that point made,' she said with mild irritation. 'But another way of making the same criticism is to substitute : "I think *of myself*, therefore I am." '

'It's not the same criticism.'

'All right, it's not the same criticism. But consider it, anyway. What's wrong with it?'

'Why . . .' Paul began. 'Something is,' he said after a moment. 'Isn't it,' he offered hesitantly, 'that the proving of thought doesn't define existence? And that' (but he still looked unconvinced of his argument) 'proving existence doesn't show where thought resides?'

Anne watched him with amusement.

'The converse wouldn't hold,' he stated with more certainty. 'You can't say, "I don't think of myself, therefore I am not." '

'Obviously,' Anne agreed. 'Unless you think of yourself you can't know whether you're not thinking of yourself. But if it can be predicated of you that you don't think of yourself, can you be proved to exist?'

'Can stones be proved to exist?'

'You're the philosopher. You tell me. *Can* stones be proved to exist?'

He was becoming heated; it annoyed him to discuss anything important with women. Either they could not, or they should not, understand. 'The idea of them exists.'

'Come,' said Anne. 'The idea of unicorns exists too.'

'Well, your "I think of myself" leads only to the conclusion that the idea of you exists.'

'Show me the unicorn who can say, "I think of myself", and I'll grant you its objective existence.'

'What's this about?' he asked. 'You're not interested in abstractions—or if you are, you've changed your skin overnight.'

'*Some* abstractions interest me. And what it's about is Roddy. Does *he* exist?'

'Of course he exists—if all the rest of us exist! He acts, doesn't he?'

'Does he?' she pondered. 'It seems to me that his forte is failing to act. But even if he does, you can't call a series of actions "Roderick Farmer". If Roddy exists, it's only by virtue of what we say or think about him. And since we are introverts, by definition primarily concerned with ourselves, what we say and think sheds more light on us than on him.'

'If we stopped talking and thinking about him, he would no longer be? You're only doing a variation on the Berkeley thing. Grant me for a moment that your hand exists. Now, if you become blind, it doesn't cease, does it, to be visible?'

'To me it does. And I'm the only person of whose existence I'm sure.'

'You still have a sense of touch,' he said wildly. 'You can feel your hand.'

'By a strange coincidence,' Anne said provocatively, 'I lost my sense of touch the same day I went blind.'

'All right,' he said. 'You're blind and deaf and dumb and tactless and can't smell. But if there's a God, your hand is still visible.'

'If there's a God—which you've always claimed not to believe—and if He can be proved—which you say He can't—He is still perfectly unknowable. *You* can't have knowledge of what *He* sees.'

He beat a retreat. 'One can't say, "God is something", only "God is". Between essence and attributes, there's . . .'

'No connexion,' Anne supplied. ' "And God said unto Moses: I AM THAT I AM." Very well; if philosophy has advanced so small a distance beyond the views held by the old mythologists of the Pentateuch, I'll meet you on your own terms, though I think myself that everything connects, if only you can find out where: Art's only a matter of making the connexions for one's audience. But "God simply is" is only another way of saying, "You can't know God"—which is my very point.'

'I'd like to see you prove that.'

'You wouldn't,' she said with a grin. 'You'd hate it. But the onus is on you, to prove that He can be known.'

'Christ!' he muttered. 'You're like all women—you twist things, you don't use words to mean the same as me.' He tried a different approach. 'Introvert and extravert are merely comparative terms. Nobody's completely the one or the other.'

'I distrust that word "merely",' Anne objected. 'Before you call them labels, let me remark that the point about labels is the differences they help to establish: plum jam, gooseberry jam, coffee, rice. Even if you get your labels muddled up, what's in the jars remains as it was. The differences themselves are absolute—like existence.'

'You'd have quite a good mind, Anne my darling, if only it had been better trained.'

'*Tu quoque*,' she observed.

He slid from the table where he had been sitting, and came over to her.

For a moment she held him off. 'I've noticed before that whenever men are losing a verbal argument they want to transfer the battle-ground to bed.'

'You're complaining?'

She moved closer.

'Existence, attributes, reality!' he said down her neck. 'Does your pretty cunt exist?' A thought struck him, and he let go of her. She withdrew a couple of paces, casting at him a demurely injured look.

'I've been thinking of what you said just now about the artist's having to make the connexions for the audience. Doesn't that contradict your theory that interpretations of reality are free, and therefore manifold?'

'No, why should it? I believe for the *artist* interpretations are manifold; but once he's chosen, bounds have been set; I don't say the critic, the audience, is free!' Anne replied.

'But if the art is Romantic?'

'Then the work possesses a variety of meanings; but if they're not experienced simultaneously, their creator has failed. I'm not at all sure, you know, whether there can ever be any useful criticism of Romantic art, with the exception of the drama. A Shakespearian play can profitably be taken apart and reassembled, but faced with Chopin or Géricault or Byron, what can anyone possibly say that both makes sense and will add to anyone's enjoyment? That's why Keats got such a bad deal: you can sound so much more intelligent attacking him than defending!'

'Surely there's been *some* relevant criticism of the Romantics?' he asked.

She shrugged. 'Can't think of any. Well, of the Romantics themselves, yes, but not of their work. Unless you go all psychological, you *can't* analyse Romanticism. It is, I suppose, a disease, and to be treated like one: you can explain the Romantic only by discussing how it differs from the norm.'

'Anne, little one? Do you regard people from the position of the artist, or the critic?'

'Depends how well I know them. Usually I can't paint my friends. Oh, you mean is the interpretation free for me, or fixed?'

He nodded.

'Fixed. It may change in the course of time, as I myself change, but at any one moment, fixed.'

'What would you do,' he asked curiously, 'if you had to paint Roddy?'

She answered slowly, and, as slowly, a grin came to her face, a nervous grin. 'If I had to paint Roddy—the picture would be Oriental in style. I'd do a group portrait of all of us, and he would be the space where all our thoughts meet. He would be the furniture, the mirrors—he would be our consciences, he would be the things each of us thinks and none of us says. He would be the surrounding air.'

Out of silence, Paul said loudly, 'For me he's so much more than that!'

'Paint him yourself, then. And don't you mean,' Anne asked, 'so much less?'

Roddy

Amargo es el labio de los que no recuerdan haber comido una fruta dulce; sordo el oído de los que no recuerdan el canto de un pájaro; ciego el ojo que al cerrarse no encuentra bajo sus párpados, la sonrisa de una cara adorable, tal vez ya muerta, o los colores del paisaje, en que fue dichoso. . . . El Paraíso fue el recuerdo de otro Paraíso. . . .

Miguel Ángel Asturias, *El Alhajadito*

Bitter is the mouth of those who do not remember having eaten a sweet fruit; dull the ear of those who do not remember the song of a bird; blind the man's eye that when it closes does not find beneath its lids the smile of a beloved face, perhaps already dead, or the colours of the landscape in which he experienced felicity. . . . Paradise was the memory of another Paradise. . . .

1

'Paint him yourself, then.' Very well: Anne's chief misapprehension lies in holding Roddy to be an extravert. I distrust all classifications that would seek to divide mankind into two groups, for there are always the uncomfortable ones who will fit in neither and who are not interested in membership of categories. Roddy, in my view, far from being an extravert, is almost invariably absorbed in the products of his own mind; but those products are of a special *genre*. He listens continuaally to mental music.

Just as all science aspires to become mathematics, so, Pater has said, 'All art constantly aspires towards the condition of music.' Alone among arts it is incapable of a didactic content. A picture may persecute, a building exhort, a book may bully. Music, like water, is content merely to exist.

I do not claim to know yet what music is, or literature, or painting. It was related to me in my school-days that if I broke water down I would discover for every part of oxygen two parts of hydrogen. I did not believe it. Experiments were devised in proof. I still did not believe. Offer your hydrogen, offer your ogygen, to a man dying of thirst in the desert, and take careful note of what he says. Reduce colour to wave-length, reduce tone and language to vibration or to the shapes traced by a pen moving across a sheet of paper; you will then have an analysis which may be scientifically true, the most faithful of inventories, but which, poetically, emotionally, in every mode comprehensible to the imagination, is not only false, not only irrelevant, not only shallow, but grotesque.

To decide what is grotesque is one way of beginning. Grotesque it is to speak of 'vibration' to anybody who has seen Janice (moving a silver pencil to the silver icy stateliness of Mozart) crouch, propped on her pillow, to jot down in her small punctilious script more than a thousand words, peruse them, omit many, add a few, amend extensively the phrasing, alter the punctuation, transpose some phrases here, two sentences there, read the whole once more through—and tear it calmly to minute pieces, before, with a wail of 'If only one could do without plot!' she at once resumes the effort to distil, from memory or intuition, from sound, from meaning, from every alert sense, a new, more sparkling, more potent perfume, whose elegance will bear no marks of the struggle and unmistakably the signature of her hand.

Grotesque to mention 'wave-length' to one who for weeks has suffered meal-times with Anne at her most sullen, sarcastic, despondent, and known her to spend the rest of the day silent and motionless, dressed in black or red sweater, shabby, baggy charcoal-and-paint-besmeared slacks, listening grimly to jazz as if to a description of her death, not even bothering to drag out her easel or pick up a sketching-block; and then, one morning—*jabot* of her emerald satin blouse trailing into her colours—through an open doorway glimpsed her exultantly painting, her hair, damp from her exertions, fuming around her brow, and her impatient brush dashing with supreme confidence in great sweeps up the canvas. And I, wanting to sleep with her, wanting to touch her hair, have gone softly away into the isolation of my study, to fix with unfriendly regard a row of useless books, jab at a pile of useless papers, ask myself why I can neither write, nor compose, nor sculpt, nor paint.

Another way to approach the task of defining an art is to pluck off all the flourishes it has acquired through the centuries, and to determine what quality its first instrument possessed. Searching back through the history of music, one eliminates harmony (obsession of the West), eliminates melody, eliminates tone; pushes past counterpoint as the rank primeval jungle is neared, to reach, at last, through thicket and swamp, the point itself: ordered sound, rhythm, the beating drum, the shrill squealing whistle, of time.

Time! Time! 'Time, gentlemen, please!' Breakfast-time, marching-time, all the pleasures, the disciplines, the tragedies, to which we submit ourselves! Of the four interwoven strands of its composition, we each select one for our peculiar concern, a noose to hang ourselves with: Anne, delving into archives, the past; Janice, deftly inventing adult fairy-tales, the future; Celia, eternity, where all her prostitutes are happily married to the first of their loves and a fountain of milk and honey always plays. Rogue males, Roddy and I choose the present—which is eccentric and ridiculous of us; for by our brutish concentration on it we waste every opportunity, dogs mumbling a bone we shall by tomorrow have left (mauled, chawed and slavered) to lie beneath the earth, the fruitful earth where soon my wife shall lie sardonically watching us to see if it will be satisfaction that we feel when, with the wind tumbling down leaves, tumbling leaves down around us, we read on a grey stone, in some wintry woe-begone cemetery, her epitaph, the frozen music of time.

It was learned by the painters long ago, the significance of Einsteinian time, strange new universe where meaning is not layered, but extends across pursued horizons. In the works of Picasso and of Braque, many profiles become one. So Newton passed light through a pyramid of glass to make his magic spectrum; so the child paints the seven colours of the rainbow on a card, threads it with string, and spins it between his fingers till, rapidly rotating, it becomes, as if miraculously, white. Late, the novelists (Huxley, in *Point Counter Point*, and then that other cosmopolitan, greatest of his time, the Anglo-Indo-Irishman, Durrell, brooding in the city built by Alexander to be Cavafy's grave) came to grips with the continuum, but still forgot one thing: that as the directions of the

153

compass, if the place where they intersect be counted, are not four but five (the Aztecs, the Maya, counted it), so to life there is an extra dimension when eternity is numbered—eternity, Always for some, for others Never.

Each escalator on which, its magnitude and scope reduced, the possible is always or never made real, rolls at a different pace. There are moments when we think we have drawn level with another of the hurtling escalators, but by the time we are sure, already the moment has gone, it is too late; and besides, we were always too far apart for clear communication to be made. It is possible, renouncing for ever the concept of equality, to strike up acquaintance with travellers before and after us on the same escalator. Many do, conveniently ignoring that the steps are ranged as parallels which, prolonged infinitely, will never meet. Others talk to mirrors, paper, shadows, tea-leaves, a manufactured God; speak out aloud, and hear—but always later—echoes replying in an empty room. Some, gazing into the eyes of a lover, find themselves staring at their own reflection, and burrow quickly closer, not to see. A few, in whom may lurk the means of redemption, by fragmentation encourage unity, smashing that they may build; or smash in order to destroy.

2

It is my belief that the days when a man's deeds were the best index to his character have long departed. Except, now, when their lives depend upon the course of action they single out, the generality of men are agreed to behave as much like one another as possible, accentuating in consequence their already distressing similarity. *Mutatis mutandis*, the same is true in the realm of ideas. Only the conversation of school-children and undergraduates has revelations to make about character or anything else; we all degenerate from our twenty-fifth year onwards, and with some the process of decay is synonymous with growth. Having met Roddy at Winchester, I know about him what I otherwise surely would not: that his thoughts are immersed in music and strategy, of which the first, being abstract, is amoral, and the second, concerned with prizes and destruction, depends upon whatever principles of morality may sway when war has been declared. Roddy, as I see him, is a clear-headed opportunist, content, and trained, to bide his time.

*

When first, a new master, I noticed him, he was a sulky boy, stiff-necked in carriage, rather heavy, but with something of the poet, however failed, about him. It was dinner; across the Hall I caught sight of him staring intently into a rounded soup spoon that he held, as if fastidiously, away from his body, and carefully tilted. Curious to know the object of his scrutiny, I picked up and examined my own spoon. Not well versed in the laws of optics, I had forgotten that the concave surface reversed one's image : the window behind my right shoulder appeared at my inverted left, and was projected till it seemed level with the spoon's upper edges. Instinctively I touched it to assure myself that, after all, the ghosted reflection was contained in the silver shining bowl. If I tipped the spoon up, I could see topsyturvy glimpses of what was happening behind, and Farmer himself seemed to be preoccupied with the observation of that fact. As I looked, he turned the spoon over— and immediately, with brutal dispatch but at the same time the completeness of an act to which his whole will was bent, dipped it into the soup until the handle alone remained dry.

The convex surface, gleaming, showed the window more sharply, and other, less well-lit objects took their place now in the background. Distortion was considerable. Mouth, chin, neck, shoulders, were reduced to insignificance, while the slope of the forehead was caricatured and the two perpendicular furrows at the bridge of my nose, tributes to eye-strain, were given stronger emphasis. Elongated, the nose itself became absurdly prominent, swelling to a great thrusting bulb.

'Don't like the soup?'

'Oh yes,' I said with a start, 'it's very good.'

My glance returned involuntarily to Farmer.

'Narcissist,' said my colleague briefly, following it. 'Never know what he's thinking.' He hesitated, and with a touch of indignation added, 'Like trying to teach a bloody statue.' Overcome, it seemed, by his own wit, he compressed his lips to maintain a suitable severity, but chortled despite himself, and then, frowning at me, choked.

*

I learned to modify all three judgements. It was disconcerting, but not dull, to instruct a boy who preferred Livy to Virgil,

Thucydides to Homer, Xenophon and Caesar to Sappho and Catullus; who read Herodotus for his *facts*; who held, about the Antonine Wall, the signal-stations on the Yorkshire coast, and the defences at Rey Cross, opinions. The boy was unteachable only because he had taught himself already everything he wished to know. Nor, once his terminology had been acquired, was his thought hard to penetrate and comprehend. He envisaged life as a campaign in which looting was forbidden because it distracted attention from the larger, no less mercenary and sordid, ends.

He was a perfectionist. He was also a psychopath. I have seen him re-copy a whole essay because of a single slip of the pen; and, less admirably, I have seen him pay a cripple to get out of his sight. Abnormalities, mistakes, defects, horrified him. Often I have wondered what he would do if he became aware of the cleft in his own mind. Commit not suicide but murder, I suspect, and that on the grand scale. He stared at a looking-glass because it presented an image, of himself, admittedly, but, with more relevance, of near-perfection, of nascent deity. If he fell in love with his sister, it would be as with a suppler, more lively, more nearly perfect, idol. There is no antidote for blasphemies and sicknesses like his.

The year Roddy won the Organ Scholarship to Oxford that he was to take up eighteen months later, the year I became uncomfortably conscious that the position he occupied in my mind was excessive and ambiguous, his father, Stephen, died. I had attended once an informal party at which the diplomat was present, and even then it had been a fascination and a shock to see an earlier rendering of the same face on a body so much slighter, to hear the same golden tones struck with greater incisiveness, and listen to a philosophy completely dissimilar coming from the same mouth. Light, insouciant, urbane, the voice was saying something about other civilisations that had ended in :

' . . . hermaphrodites flirting with hermaphrodites. When the Athenians accused Socrates of corrupting the youth, they really meant he was corrupting the girls; and naturally if the corruption of the girls was visible there had to be a culprit.'

*

157

'Boy needs keeping an eye on. Taking it too calmly.'

I nodded. We both watched Roddy inspect its concave surface and, apparently satisfied, dip into the bowl of soup his spoon. He had particularly asked to be allowed to await the end of term in the usual way, absenting himself only for the funeral.

'He has no other relations?' I inquired.

'Mother's dead. Sister's gallivantin' about in Greece with the ward. Not going to tell them yet. Spoil their vacation. Take it hard, women.'

'Who'll have charge of Roderick till his majority?' I inquired.

'Uncle, so it seems. Matter of fact they're inviting you down for a few weeks—separate letter for you here. Know you're the only person who understands the boy. Go, I s'pose?'

'I shall have to, if Farmer's willing.'

The old man eyed me and passed the envelope over. 'Better ask him.'

*

Just then I happened to be very busy. That I was in the running, and the favoured candidate, for the housemastership due to fall vacant when the old man retired was plain. If I stayed I should have to marry. I was not sure if I wished to marry, and I was not sure if I wished to stay. These preoccupations engaged part of my mind; the rest was given to the management of house affairs, so many of which already devolved upon me. The funeral was over—as indeed it was best it should be—before I broached to Roddy the subject of his uncle's letter. By that time it was common knowledge that the money had been bequeathed to the boy's sister, reputed to be of a religious turn. I found the situation faintly comical, but could well imagine that Roddy himself possessed another view of it.

As I descended the stairs the door of his room stood open, quite wide. For once there was no sound of music, and perhaps for that very reason the silence had an indefinably oppressive quality. To my first glance the study appeared deserted, and I was about to retreat to my own room once more when I heard footsteps within, and, pausing on the landing, saw Roddy, clad in a brown dressing-gown that gave him the aspect of a Franciscan friar, cross, holding sponge-bag and tooth-glass, with a towel slung over his arm, to the full mirror above the chimney-piece.

His face, reflected there and, under the strong yellow light, visible, though but indistinctly, even to my poor sight, seemed as usual to show very little expression. Closer, I should probably have noticed the golden hair brushed stiffly forward, and the unexpectedly dark lashes that guarded, like spines, his always staring eyes; but the angle at which the mirror was slanted would have allowed a stranger only to guess at the patrician regard, the haughtiness of the brow, focusing his attention rather upon the wedged cheeks and the thick fleshy lips. The likeness of the lower part of Roddy's face, when glimpsed in isolation, to a prize-fighter's came, after all this time, as an enormous shock.

Index finger of his left hand still crooked through the string of the sponge-bag, after a moment he set down the glass of water previously held in his right, and, gripping the mirror closely, tilted it towards him, bending forward to gaze, with heightened intentness, into his own eyes. I could now see none of the image, hidden as it was by his shoulders and the back of his head.

The towel slid to the floor. He replaced the mirror, and took up first one, then another, photograph, both of which he proceeded carefully to compare with the image before him, now visible to me once again. The first photograph, which, from previous visits to his room, I took to be of his now deceased father, he put slowly back on the shelf; the second, and larger, he tapped deliberately against the wall, with about the same degree of force one would use to break open a boiled egg. Stooping, with the handle of his tooth-brush he shovelled the pieces of fallen glass together against the sponge-bag, and flicked them, his manner leisurely, controlled and precise, into the waste-paper basket.

Then he turned and, as if contemplatively, lifted the tumbler. With extraordinary violence he dashed its contents all over the gleaming reflection. We both watched the liquid course, then trickle, down. Having thrust the wet tumbler into the sponge-bag, and transferred the latter to his right hand, he swung the bag back, and brought it with the same violence across his own image, which shivered to fragments. The wooden mirror, with a few jagged, curving slivers of glass still adhering to it, toppled and fell with a smack into the fire-place. While he was bending to pick it up, I turned quickly and mounted, two at a time, the stairs. I was still explaining on the internal telephone that he ought to be moved to the sanatorium without delay when I heard another crash. Another came, and another. By the time assistance had arrived, not a window in his corridor was left intact.

3

We took a late train, dining on the journey, and were met at the station by the chauffeur. As, in the gloom, our steps, markedly out of unison, scrunched after our luggage up the path, I could see very little of Godfrey Cunningham's house; but a faint ghostly fragrance, as of honeysuckle, gave me a shadowy idea of what to expect. Slight and courtly, Roddy's uncle received us wearing a plum-coloured corduroy smoking-jacket, the first such garment I had seen, immediately attractive to me. His wife appeared a moment later, bluff, kind, broad-busted, peremptory, in a dress rather more feminine, both in style and hue, than suited her temperament, a characteristic I had remarked several times before in women of her background and her age. What we were to do was by her made unmistakably clear to us: to take a bath, come downstairs for a hot drink, and as soon as possible retire to bed.

Vigorously scrubbing myself in the steamy bathroom, where there guttered a paraffin lamp of lustrous heavy silver, I noted the spotless basins, the taps where my reflection, distorted and bulging, glimmered back at me, the rough good towels warming on the racks. Soon I tapped on Roddy's door, but found his room empty, and vapour still issuing from another deserted bathroom, across the landing. The contents of the bookcases dotted about had as 'period' a flavour as the rest of the house: early Masefield, W. H. Davies—to my delight, the complete works of Edward Thomas—and then, as I descended the stairs, light-weight fiction: Anthony Hope, Angela Thirkell, Edgar Wallace, Conan Doyle.

Dry, aglow, feeling eminently civilised, I entered the room where three heads were silhouetted against another of the heavy silver lamps, and found Roddy desultorily talking with his relations. Before him, its surface puckered with skin, stood a glass of chocolate. Perhaps because of the fatigue that follows travelling, I regarded it a moment too long.

'Roddy prefers it like that,' Mrs Cunningham observed, and indicated a chair. 'So funny.'

It was a rap over the knuckles; I accepted it in silence, recognising that from now on I must watch my step. She arose, and brought me from the kitchen a taller glass, which was still frothing, and evidently hot. I stood up to take it from her. She set it down near me, with a gracious shake of the head, but the smile she then turned on me said that to remember always to rise for her would be expedient.

'May I try out the piano?' inquired Roddy, putting down his glass.

'Certainly. It was tuned for you only a few days ago. Take the other lamp from the kitchen.'

When his nephew was gone, Godfrey Cunningham said quietly, 'What sort of shape is he in?'

'Not good, sir,' I replied, accommodating my vocabulary to his. 'The doctor seemed to think him well enough to travel, but I wasn't altogether easy about it.'

He nodded, and finished his chocolate. Still pensively holding the glass, he said: 'One thing I wanted to tell you, Paul. Be yourself, and enjoy your holiday. You're not here to keep an eye on him.' He added, 'He respects you; we're relieved to find you as you are, for usually his taste isn't of the happiest.'

Mrs Cunningham stared at me.

I felt profoundly uncomfortable. Music came from the other room, dropping into the darkness as into the basin of a fountain, formal, chill, remote; and the subject was relinquished, never to be taken up again. The piece over, we bade one another good night and went upstairs, into a different silence. Outside the windows it was counterpointed by the branches and leaves that justled, rubbing themselves together, with a sound like taffeta brushing over long corridors, and by a rainy wind full of the cries of birds. Inside, it was deep as a well, reverberating, echoing.

I knew instinctively that Mrs Cunningham placed biscuits by the beds only of those guests she did not like, and though they were my favourites, whole-meal coated with chocolate, I refrained from touching them. Vowing that tomorrow I would devote myself to winning her over, I slid blissfully under the crumbless lavender-scented sheets.

*

It was early when I awoke, but the others were already up. Grapefruit, glistening and crusty with moist sugar, awaited me; with a brisk 'Good morning' my hostess bustled starchily across the room in a flowered house-coat, set beside me an alternative dish, of creamy porridge, and pushed over the table more cream, butter, brown sugar, before losing herself in the morning news. Poached eggs followed, yellow as the sunshine dancing on the white walls; then toast and streaky golden orange marmalade, with coffee, strong, and scalding hot. Mrs Cunningham withdrew before I had finished, and a little later, through the window, I saw her striding purposefully across the garden, armed with, and snapping, a large pair of scissors, and clad now in a mauve linen dress somewhat at variance with her complexion.

There were already flowers in the room, but they were dying: a massive bowl of crystal, rimmed with silver, that one could hardly see for the roses crammed within. One white petal had already parted from its fellows; a second, drooping, shrivelled to a point, was ready to detach itself, and, as I bent towards it, it fluttered in hesitating spirals to the floor. After it toppled another, violently. So a mountaineer, in his fall, twists, and drags with him a companion, tethered to life by the same rope. I had a queer mental image of struggling with Roddy on a peak of ice such as the ones we had seen the previous day in a film of a Hemingway story; as our feet slithered and lost ground, I experienced also a wild temptation to smash the crystal bowl, cold against my hands, to smithereens. Fortunate that I'm not to be made the boy's keeper! I thought, picking up the fallen petals.

In the kitchen, the sight of a woman at work sweeping the floor assured me that at least I need not offer to help with the washing-up in order to ingratiate myself with Mrs Cunningham. We looked at each other; the woman smiled, and I nodded, before I passed through the doorway into the garden.

To the left of the house, velvety orange and brown wallflowers were clumped; particoloured sweet-williams (cerise-and-white, white-and-magenta, several shades of pink); gillyflowers, with their aroma of cloves; pansies, or heart's-ease; love-in-a-mist; columbines. Then the garden began to escape its formal pattern, and into the grass nasturtium trailed its dark heart-shaped leaves. Demure wallflowers hid by the fence again, meaning the sunshine of a whole summer. Nearer the house, and to the right, was a kitchen-garden, lavish with herbs. Clary grew here, blue chicory, costmary, burnet and chervil; borage, tart tarragon, and feathery, umbelliferous parsley.

'Shallots,' I said aloud, 'from Ascalon.'

Close, I heard laughter, and looking up saw a sunlit visage, silver hair, a mauve dress, approaching through the trees.

'Quite right, young man,' said Mrs Cunningham, with the first signs of approval she had yet shown. 'And full marks' (holding up a sprig of it) 'if you can tell me the derivation of "rosemary".'

'I'd always associated it with the Virgin.' (Ought I, I wondered, to have said 'the *Blessed* Virgin'?) 'Rosemary for remembrance; rosemary and rue . . . I can't produce what you want, I'm afraid.'

'You won't risk a guess?'

'*Ros marinus!*' I exclaimed with sudden inspiration. 'Marine dew.'

At which moment, Roddy sauntered across from under the

trees, and I was unable to learn whether I had been wise or
not to deprive Mrs Cunningham of her triumph.

'Ask my profligate nephew to show you the rest of the
garden,' she said with a wave of the scissors. 'I'll see you both
at lunch. Gather any rosebuds that please you, except the
damasks—no loss, because others are prettier, but they make
the best scent.'

Our morning thus disposed of, we strolled over the lawns,
and were soon deep again in roses.

'Wonderful garden!' I said, having long ago decided that
inanity was permissible in Roddy's presence.

'Yes,' he responded. 'Wonderful.'

And I felt that not only it, but I, had been for ever dismissed.

Apparently conscious himself that he had been more than
usually abrupt, he struggled to atone. 'Gloire de Dijon,' he
offered with an auctioneer's gesture, 'and Maiden's Blush. I
think this one is Lady Forteviot . . .'

'I know them all perfectly well,' I said, laughing. 'It's the
Rose of Provence.'

The gathered whiteness, with delicacies of shade, like
packed ice and snow, but so much softer, and rather matt
than sparkling, was satiny above the shot silk of translucent
leaves whose veins showed dark in the sun.

Why does no one except Anne wear satin nowadays? Anne
in copper satin, Anne in jade green, Anne in buttercup yellow,
with her hair rumpled as she smokes over a painting not going
well . . . can I be falling in love with her, after this long time,
again?

Roddy glanced surreptitiously at his watch. I caught his eye.
'Don't you like them?' I asked.

He stared about with a helpless air, fingering the ragged
hems at calyx and stalk of the moss rose. 'They're so—so
untidy!' he said. He gestured at the wild irregular Boursaults.
I looked around, and for a moment saw them through his
eyes: saw unkempt spiky roses with thorns like the long
rapacious beaks of parrots.

The moment passed, and before me there were again tight
tea-roses, small, reticent, their petals touched with the coolest
fire; roses dragon-red, still as a gipsy who, having danced, wraps
her flaring skirts about her; twining buds, inseparable each from

the other; swelling full-blown roses, goblet and navel, labyrinthine their corollas, convoluted in inviolable whorls; deepenings and fadings where shell-like colours blent, petals one tried to unravel with the gaze; a bough in our way that I held back and released after us so that it sprung back, swung, swung again, gently nodding with mastered resilience, scattering a virtuoso melody of petals over the lawn, *arpeggio*, *cadenza*, and after it silence, before the next movement should begin.

We walked back, through roses, and the petals of roses, and their leaves, past the kitchen-garden and down the path out of the grounds, feet crunching again, out of unison, over the gravel. Unwillingly I suggested we should part company until lunch-time. Roddy agreed without enthusiasm. His manner would have been the same if I had suggested we remain together all day.

*

My eyes flinched at first before the sudden rush of brilliant light and shadow. The sun was pouring down like golden rain, and the whole sky glowed, transparent. Again there were roses: ramblers, dog-roses, musk. On the hedges woodbine rang riot, and under them the grass was starred with celandines. The berries on the brambles were still green and polished, but on the huge horse-chestnut, down the drive, behind sweltering sticky fans of emerald leaf the flambeaux were already almost burned out. As I returned, my eyes, sharper now, noticed tufts of wool caught on the barbed-wire fences; hens ran creeking across the road in front of me, and I resolved to visit the farm if possible, after lunch.

When I entered the house, the darkness was a cool shock like the feel of the sea on one's skin, after the heat and the dust.

'Good, you're in time for some sherry,' said Godfrey Cunningham. 'Unlike my nephew, who will undoubtedly . . .'

But Roddy, appearing at that moment, was also able to appreciate Amontillado's light hue and sombre taste. We ate enormously : iced cucumber soup; beef, in solid mighty slices, with horse-radish freshly scraped from the root; then syllabubs, compounded of whisky, Marsala, cream, castor sugar, and above all lemon, its zest and juice; cheese, finally—*Notre Dame de Carentan*—with murrey-coloured Burgundy.

'You mustn't think we live in this degenerate style usually,' his uncle said, 'but when Roddy's here it's Christmas and Hallowe'en, harvest home and the *Lupercalia* all in one.' We drank coffee. The brandy burned in our throats. Through the sunlight curled the thin sweet fragrance of Turkish cigarettes.

'Would you like to see the farm?' asked Mrs Cunningham, her animosity gone. 'We don't work it ourselves, having no talent for that sort of thing; but we're always honoured guests.'

Delighted, I accompanied her. Roddy, to my surprise, followed, albeit morosely. It was good to savour the warm smell of dung; to watch cows crumping their fodder; to slap their flanks and to feel their dry tongues tickle the palm of my hand.

'And the sheep?' I asked impetuously.

'Through the gate, look.'

There they were, marvellously silly creatures, scampering with imbecile prudence away down the field on seeing me, their legs thin, black-stockinged, like old and maiden ladies.

Suddenly I looked back in search of Roddy, and saw him fixedly regard a trough of pigs, the litter clambering over the backs of one another and their dam to swill, intently, their wash.

'He'll sort himself out again with his music. I've seen him before like this when his plans haven't worked out,' said Mrs Cunningham, interpreting my glance.

When his plans haven't worked out. . . .

I studied her innocent shrewd eyes, and she moved restlessly away, gazing after the sheep.

'You're rather a hero to the boy, although he mayn't show it.'

I was silent.

'You're hardly the usual town-bred ignoramus?' she said.

With a laugh, 'I wanted to be a farmer, once,' I replied.

'And your parents were agin it?' she asked, smiling.

'They suggested it was easier to enter a university on Classics than agriculture. Besides, a *course* on agriculture would be so unromantic, they thought. They could bear the idea of the muck-heap, but not of nitrates.'

She laughed in her turn.

'And then everyone told me that as I had studied Classics it would be a waste to farm: if I had wanted all along to take up farming, why, I ought to have read that subject in the beginning. "Agriculture is a science, nowadays." '

She thought I was attacking my parents, and she may have been right. 'Not reasons, really?' she said.

'No, not reasons,' I responded, 'excuses. I've always been a dilettante. As a dilettante rustic, no doubt I should have come to ruin.'

Irritably she brushed away a buzzing fly. 'You may do that yet,' she remarked. 'I've no patience with people who can't make up their minds.'

Cautiously, feeling uncouth again, I manœuvred till we were back on a more general topic. There is no room for egocentrics or their irony among the English upper classes. After a while Mrs Cunningham went indoors, and I joined Roddy.

'If only,' he exclaimed, 'I could always live on a farm, or near one!'

'Perhaps . . .' Realising the indelicacy of what I had been about to say, I did not finish the sentence, but he understood.

'They'll leave it to my sister. People always do.' Spontaneously he retreated from dangerous ground. 'I'm going to practise, this afternoon. You can amuse yourself, can you?'

'Of course.'

*

So I set off, in another direction, past fields where the sifting wind riffled the grain, the darnel, riffled the corn-flowers, riffled the somnolent poppies; through a grove of birches; past more fields, to where, shouldering the sky circled by kestrels in the hot afternoon, the downs humped squatly into the distance. Here the sun was naked: pods of broom shot open with a sudden dry rattle, startling the birds; thistle-down, and the fluff from dandelion clocks, floated lazily in the air. I lay watching the spiders scuttle, listening to the drowsy crickets, till towards tea-time, when, following a path that took me over dunched damp soil where cowslips grew, and meadowsweet, below a waterfall cascading like bundles of brown silk I came to a bridge from whose height I could see the house.

'I know where *you've* been!' said the maid. 'And you're just in time for some tea.'

My shoes were stolchy with mud. I scraped them thoroughly before making my way through the kitchen, whose glossy orange floor and neat shelves invariably smelled of turkey and redcurrants and polish and loving care. Through the hot, crusty toast the butter seeped, swimming in golden pools, to be overspread luxuriously with cherry jam, or honey that dripped amber from the comb. The open windows showed skies now brindled, and welcomed the aromas of dusk.

Afterwards, with Roddy still at practice, his uncle working in the study, and his aunt away on a visit in the village, I became acutely conscious of the ticking clock. There ought to have been perfect peace, here in this peaceful house. Instead, alone with my own thoughts, I was both agitated and discontent. Time and the movement of the four seasons were visible; out of the window, the present was slipping away into other afternoons, other evenings, other nights, other years. The maid came in, to draw the great rust curtains and light the lamps. She departed, the diversion was gone, again I was trying to think of anything but my relationship with the golden-haired evil boy, to whom I was, it seemed, a 'hero' with whom he had no desire to converse.

*

Days passed. Autumn had begun to arrive, foxing the leaves. In the evenings I talked with Godfrey Cunningham of many things, over the sheen of stiff linen where silver and glass gleamed; or, after dinner, watching light glow rubescent in our port, amid furniture built for comfort (shiny, cherished, smelling of polish), surrounded by mellow shadows and reflections just as kindly.

'But they're dead now,' he said quietly. 'Chesterton and Belloc, all the great boomers.'

He sighed, and, bringing out a little round casket, swiftly offered me snuff. I looked at him curiously, courtly old man whose smoking-jacket would be worn by no one after him,

169

courtly old man dying through the years, and a world dying with him. After the briefest hesitation, I took a pinch, to please him. A twinkle was in his eyes as he watched me, and when he saw my expression change he burst into a hearty laugh. 'Not the usual pepper!' he cried. 'But you won't know what it is!'

'I believe, sir, I do!' I retorted.

He was dubious. 'Well?'

'Attar of roses....' I mused.

'Go on,' he encouraged, his whole face radiant.

'Maccabaw,' I said at last. 'Or maccaboy, if you prefer. It's from Martinique.'

We were close friends.

But autumn had come over the wind-drunken tawny landscapes, to tumble in bundles russety leaves; to build its crackling filemot bonfires autumn had come. Smoke shifted like dreams, or greyish clouds with the sun shimmering and glistering through them, or dust. Dustwhirls, dustdrifts, where smouldering leaves hung suspended and in surges the wild flames leaped, coiled sinuously in the garden, catching the breath and making the eyes smart. The damsons and the plums were ripe; the wasps sizzled; in the bonfires was the odour of once and future roses.

When we had gone, white and brumous would come the chill sparkle of winter. Our images were distorted in the taps here for the last time; and soon I would never see the courtly old man or his like again.

4

In the following year there was no scene, no revelation, no crisis. There was no explosion: only the acridity of a match scraped too rapidly along the box, flaring—with a flash, with a sputter—and in a wavering slow trail of smoke consuming itself. The smoke lingered after the match was burned out. Not liking the look or the smell, I went to another place: I left Roddy, and Winchester; I came to London, where Janice became my wife.

Whether reality exists or not is a matter of belief. Most men doubt heaven, from time to time; a few doubt hell; the born sceptic doubts the earth. Because for him there is no contrast between reality and illusion, the sceptic tends to be more tolerant than others are: the effect of reducing to nil the necessary is perforce to widen the imagination's scope.

Crimes are committed, and sometimes men are tried for them. 'Prisoner at the bar, do you plead guilty . . .?' The poor fellow standing in the dock has to answer this absurd question. Of course he is guilty; we are all guilty; but is that a reason why he, before another, should pay the penalty for the particular offence with which he is charged? So, trying above all not to wet himself, he claims, with the support of his counsel—who is paid for that very support—to be white as driven snow, and the pomp and pageantry of the law assumes guiltlessness to be his condition, until the contrary shall be proved. Harrowed by the reverberating falsity of so simple an hypothesis, prosecuting counsel ruffles up, his robes bristling, to denounce the defendant's temerity. If, as is probable, the creature in the dock had up to this moment possessed a private life, unwashed it will be brandished before him. By the time, in a flurry of impersonal, relentless indignation, counsel can bring himself to be seated once more, not a man amongst his hearers but will be convinced that the defendant's iniquity far exceeds any crime for which he could be called to account. Feeling cleaner at the very thought, 'Already he looks more like the rogue he is!' they say to themselves. But the defence counsel's hour will also come. 'White as snow'—'black as pitch'—a suspicion will creep across the jury's minds, such of them as have minds, that since, according to the logic of their faith, both assertions cannot, simultaneously at least, be true, perhaps neither of them is. They have no leisure, even if they would, to examine their faith or logic. Up and down will wobble the scales of justice, in search of equilibrium, and a verdict must be reached.

Found guilty, the murderer will continue to be with eagerness dissected; the morality of his victim will be questioned; dinners will grow cold through agitation at the villain's, the martyr's, the hero's fate. 'I should have done the same in his place!' rebellious voices cry who did not admit it while the trial was on. I too, and all of us, would have done the same in his place; and all of us would have hanged for it; but that is not the point, for we managed, not being in his place, to escape the law, this time. Acquitted, escaping the law, this time, the thief walks out into the cameras and the daylight with all his thievery about him, to find he cannot obtain a job, he cannot rid himself of an unpleasant feeling that his family's reception of him is unwarrantably cold. Reality is a matter of belief; and whether I, given the opportunity, would be a paederast, whether Roddy is by taste or practice homosexual, are questions to which there may be many different answers.

*

What interests me is to learn other people's. I should like, for instance, to see Anne's portrait of Roddy and hear its title: 'Adonis'? 'Narcissus'? 'Portrait of a Lover'? 'The Music Master at a Suburban Comprehensive School'?

'The picture would be Oriental in style. I'd do a group portrait of all of us. . . . He would be the furniture, the mirrors— he would be our consciences, he would be the things each of us thinks and none of us says. He would be the surrounding air.'

In the Orient there is no belief in symmetry. Imperfection is cherished. Flaws do not insult the gods in the manner of things unmarred. The warped frail faces that are Utamaro and Kiyonaga testify in Japan to a creed for which right and left are different entities and not congruent; where lines must lose themselves rather than be straight; where curves shall never be true. Frameless, with neither beginning nor end, the canvases, or the silks, where, sketched exquisitely with a dry brush, the shades and spectres of bamboo, lotus, chrysanthemums appear, permit in China the occurrence of growth, allow the entry of time. Untroubled by perspective, in Persia, in India, figures do not walk, but float in air. Space, which to our poverty-stricken, affluent minds means emptiness, is to the Oriental somewhere for the gaze to rest; like a pause in music, it supplies a haven in which thought, or silence, or eternity, may breathe and be developed.

Anne's picture of Roddy would therefore be disturbing. I have known what it is, for him to be the furniture: the old good shiny furniture that smelled of polish, under lamplight; or the school-rooms stained with ink, the chalk squeaking shrilly over a dusty blackboard, the chipped desks where generations of names, of ribaldry, or the annals of courtship, were carved; a hall where dishes clattered and to the scrapings of chairs a hubbub of young voices made the head ache; a study . . . a study . . . a study . . . rooms filled with lassitude and sun. I have left places because Roddy was the furniture. I have gone away from stillnesses where Roddy was the things

173

each of us guiltily thought, and, superstitiously, none of us ever said. I have avoided eyes in which I saw reflected my own cogitations: saw the knowledge that, when Janice is dead, Celia may accept me, and Roddy may propose to Anne. I do not like the idea of his proposing to Anne. It hurts me, to think of her reply.

The surrounding air has been Roddy, and I have left it. He has been crackling branches, of thorn, or ash. In a country garden he has been the flames of fires which, as they billowed and surged and, twisting, eddied, might by a disordered imagination easily be taken for the fires of hell. Wasps; ripe plums; roses, he has been, dying across the evening; falling petals, fallen leaves; autumn, and the first frosts of winter. He has been every slammed lid, he has been migraine, each pulsation, each throb and torment jogging the head. In class-rooms where I have droned into the summer about the homo-sexuality of the Greeks ('effete,' I have said, 'effeminate, the end of an empire') his golden eyes have stared back at me and he has been the air through which I have driven speech to eliminate the questions silence might learn to put.

It is an infatuation, for a totally unworthy object, I have told myself. It is an infatuation dating from years (how many years?) ago. It is a physical obsession whose consummation you would abhor. Roddy is evil. You know he is evil. Evil the eyes are, blank and young and cold. Blank, cold, young, beautiful, the eyes have stared back at me and I have drowned.

Sometimes when she works at a portrait Anne goes to a mirror and takes on her face, uncannily, the expression she is about to paint. I do not want to see Roddy's expression or its lack on Anne's face. I do not want Anne to marry him, or paint of him any pictures. I wish she did not see him in mirrors, or the air, or dreams.

At our party the other night, listening, talking, laughing sometimes, but usually immobile and expressionless, he was in all the mirrors wherever I turned.

5

Anne saw them first. Her immediate advance gave me leisure
in which to stop, to watch; as they stood poised against the
doorway, to hold their image in such fashion as I might have
held, turning it over, a photograph.

How long I stood watching them I don't know. A second,
a thousand years? Neither, if I came forward then to play
the host, does any memory persist with me of what any of
us said. If I came forward, if I stayed where I was, whatever
we did, whatever we said, would have made no difference to
the situation that existed that evening and had always existed,
in which, throughout the centuries, all four of us, and Janice,
would remain involved: exchanging partners, or keeping them
the same; disguised, wearing black velvet dominoes; or in our
usual manner, with faces bare; pirouetting, bowing, curtsey-
ing, or motionless; in a ritual, self-parodying stillness, or
in a dance.

The second that just passed you was time present. Look!
There! Did you see it? Did you hear it? Did you taste and

touch and smell it? You did not. It was pretty, but you were too late. Reality, I sometimes think, is like that: like time present; like a Palladian façade I once almost saw as I passed it in a car.

How do I know I passed it? I do not. Guide-books give its position; I can mark its locality on a map. The other occupant of the car said, with reproach, that it had been there and he had seen it—'Look!' he said. 'Missed it.'

When I was a little boy, the other little boys used to say 'Look!' (pointing); and on several occasions, while I was look-ing, they hit me in the stomach. Now, when anyone points and says 'Look!' I politely neglect to do as he suggests. It is hard to unlearn what has been discovered about the world in childhood.

So far as my knowledge of him went, the other man in the car was as veracious as the rest of us. He had no more reason for deceit than, to take a convenient example, the little boys. Nevertheless, like them, he might have lied. I do not know. Other people say reality is there. Myself, I am not sure. I have met several different kinds of illusion.

And if I remembered what we said—if we said anything—and if I remembered it precisely, word for word, I would still not swear to anybody that those and no others were the words that, if we spoke, we spoke. Memory has many tricks. It has played most of them on me before.

But what I *think* I think I remember is that in all the mirrors, all the evening, I saw Roddy and Celia, together or alone; in all the mirrors, all the evening, I saw Anne. All the evening, in all the mirrors, I saw myself; myself flashing in the mirrors; and Anne; myself, all the evening, and Roddy, glimpses; in all the mirrors, myself and Celia; or Celia and Roddy, or Celia and Anne, or, all the evening, in all the mirrors—bright—dark —gleaming—shadowed—Anne and Roddy.

At one point too, that evening—the evening when I think we had a party—I saw, very clearly (although clarity, I know, is comparative; and indeed when I say 'very' I may be making more obscure what was already, like everything else, most chaotic, most confused), I saw, very clearly I say, and in spite, unless it was because, of being at the time not completely sober, that Roddy was talking with a girl, whom I seemed to

176

recollect having met when, to the extent I have ever worked, I was working as a 'literary' journalist who reviewed exhibitions of so-called art.

I saw Roddy and the girl in a mirror.

She was an attractive girl, by which I mean that on seeing her I started thinking about bed and it is probable that if I had spoken to her about bed she would not have replied with something about principles. She might have said no, but if she had said no it would have been to me, not to the idea of fornication. For some reason I associated her with Anne. Perhaps I associated her with Anne because Anne too never talks about the wickedness of fornication. I sometimes suspect, since she possesses morals, of a sort (the sort that goes with believing more things in the world are bad than good), that she did not consider fornication wicked. If so, it may only be because she possesses an extraordinary capacity for falling in love. I have noticed that even the most candid and enlightened women like to convince themselves that love and bed mean the same—as, when either is sought with sufficient frequency and perseverance, tends with the passage of time to become true.

Roddy was unusually animated. Whatever his relationship with the girl—and I balked at speculating thereon—it was close enough to allow the speech of both to be intense and, if not angry, at least vehement. The impression they gave was markedly one of intrigue.

There is nothing like alcohol for creating melodrama, actual or imaginary. I recognised at that moment that I was probably drunk. I wanted, all the same, to discover who the girl was, and found myself standing questioningly in front of Anne almost before I knew I had been seeking her. She was talking with Celia. I turned and looked again at Roddy, but the girl was no longer at his side; coquetting, or trying to coquette, with him instead was a colleague of mine, whimsical, consciously gracious, every kind of middle-aged snob, whom Anne had long ago privately dubbed 'the Blight'.

Following the direction of my eyes, Anne exclaimed at me for not ordering things better, and bore down on the group in which they stood. My opportunity lost, I found myself now, to my great distress, alone with Celia.

Absurdly, the first remark that entered my head was 'How like Roddy you are!' Yet I knew women were no more pleased to be told they resembled their brothers than their brothers would be to hear of resembling them.

We had to be inept. We had to be inadequate. Undone, like her, by silences, I cast about for polite, innocuous conversation that would keep us out of the whirlpools and the howling void till I could reasonably make my excuses and depart; but inquiringly, perhaps because of those silences, she lifted her face.

I bent to examine it, in a moment losing my equilibrium both mentally and physically. Hand against the wall to keep myself on my feet—or for protection against her?—or to hem her in?—I tried to regain some semblance, however delusive, of calm, of balance, of sanity.

Our lips began to offer each other words again that our ears cautiously tested and allowed to pass.

'... don't often see you here?'

'... work still going well?'

'... promotion?'

'... promotion.'

'... promotion! Would you care to have some punch?'

At last, none too soon, deliverance came. 'Oh, look, Anne wants you, I think.'

Across the room, eyes rolling, Anne mimed eating an outdrawn strand of hair. With complete composure I regarded her. Then, in one of those astonishing, apocalyptic, world-shaking moments of transcendental alcoholic vision, I saw, with dread, with rapture, with stupefied delight, how utterly delectable women were—*all* women: Anne, Celia, Janice, the girl who was now with Roddy again, the Blight. . . .

In my arms Anne was each one of them, deliciously: their lips, their throat and their mouth and, in shivering slow vibrations, their tongue; watched suddenly in the mirrors by Roddy, their shoulders, their breasts (how astounding was the perfection of their shoulders, their breasts!); the anguish with which the hidden part of their body, which my body with aching anguish sought, sought, distraught, the hidden responding corresponding part in me. Voices, colliding, smashed and clashed around us; trembling, Anne was sheltered in my arms; reeling, the room straightened out, watched in the mirrors by Roddy, and we were in the bedroom : serious, tentative—shy, suddenly—looking at each other and seeing no one else, but only, with specific, particularised desire, each other, ourselves, Anne Rivers, Paul Hawkes.

The light from the doorway outlined her head in three-quarter profile; her face, tilted upwards, became burnished, her hair, the slant of her cheek, caressed with burnished light. She was turned a little from me, her features hidden, made mysterious, by the enveloping dark. I was allowed only glimpses, suggestions : a hint of curving cheek, curving brow, the curving lashes of her downcast eyes, her pose for a moment so lovely I caught my breath. In the darkened mirror I saw, fleetingly (but it could not really have been), Roddy and Celia, like cousins, or twins, or a brother and sister, photographed in the doorway, then Anne was saying, her voice husky, shaken, tones deeper, something I did not understand about love and jealousy and happiness, and we moved farther into the silent dark room where jealousy lurked, and love, and I asked her, unsteadily, what happiness was, and whether she did not find it, sometimes, when she ceased to look for it, with me?

Duologue five

'Less—more—what's the difference?' Paul asked.

'A big one, I should have thought,' said Anne, her tone dry.

'But,' he persisted, 'what do the words *mean*?'

She sighed. 'As much as any others.'

'What others?' he demanded. 'Freedom? Justice? Mercy? Love?'

She made no audible response.

'Love?' he repeated. 'What does love mean? Didn't you say once, little Anne, you'd always love me?'

'No, I'm sure I didn't,' she said emphatically. 'Love's a word I very seldom use; and I learned long ago that "always" is far out of my range.'

'You may not have said it in so many words. But wasn't it implied?'

Weary suddenly, she shrugged. 'I'm not responsible for how anyone construes the things I don't say. Even when I met you,' she added, 'there was another man's taste in my mouth.'

'I thought it was the taste of the previous one, not the next in the line!'

'You're bad for me,' she declared. 'We're bad for each other. It's no one's fault.'

'Anne, don't let's try to justify ourselves. There *is* no justification. Is there any need to talk of what can't be mended, the broken things neither of us can patch up or replace?'

Sorry beyond words, she came into his arms, but, even in moving towards him, insisted to herself that this was not love; that it might be pity, or affection, desire, or the understanding that comes with shared misfortune, but it was not, it would never be, love. And knew, at the same time, that love it assuredly was : of a different kind, perhaps, of a different worth, perhaps, of a different quality, but love, as much as any of the loves with which she had ever been exhausted, had ever been seared and blistered and burned.

'I should have been born a female pirate!'

'No, you're very gentle.'

'The gentleness of the violent. The gentleness of the damned. The thing to bear in mind,' she said, touching with her lips his hair, 'is that I am irredeemably promiscuous. It's worth remembering, worth accepting, because in the end it may provide some comfort.'

'You don't regret any of your experiences?' he asked curiously.

'Of sex? No more than a man. No more than you.' Nevertheless she considered. 'I don't regret,' she qualified, 'the ones whose surname I never learned, but' (she laughed, with returning exuberance, unashamedly) 'I have qualms sometimes about those whose first name I have forgotten.'

He shook his head. 'Anne, Anne!'

She said, slowly, but, as the words followed one another, with a growing urgency : 'There was a time, long ago, when I may have said "always", and talked of love. While that time lasted, I meant it, I meant every word. How was I to know that today and tomorrow are different things? There are people every minute who stand in churches and swear, *meaning* it, *believing* it, 'Till death us do part". But I, when I look at my old school books I don't recognise the signature

I must once have written there.' She became defensive. 'Yet don't you see, Paul, it's always been the same love?'

'In so many pieces?' he asked. 'So shattered, and so marred?'

'You remember that book on early Greek philosophy you lent me? It says there that the substance of a flame is always changing, yet the flame itself is what we call a "thing". The quantity changes, the substance changes, but there's always something that's recognisably one; just as, in the Buddhist scriptures, King Milinda came to the conclusion that if a lamp was lit, to stay burning all the night, though the flame of the first watch and the second and the last was not identical, yet there was only one lamp, and because of that lamp the light could go on shining to the end of the darkness.' She paused, searching for a cigarette. 'Parallels,' she said vaguely, striking the match.

He was interested. 'Ye-es. Vasubandhu says something similar : that when a flame wanders along a piece of wood' (they both regarded the match) 'what we call "flame" is only a series of flame-moments.' His tone altered, becoming faintly malicious. 'Likewise your soul wanders in the place of birth and death—Samsara—if you're attached to your soul and agree to wander in Samsara.'

She shivered. 'I hate the word "wander"!'

He knew it. ' "Raging waves of the sea," ' he quoted, ' "foaming out their own shame; wandering stars, to whom is reserved the blackness of darkness for ever." There, with all the authority of the Unholy Scriptures, you have your fate. Take warning!'

She cried out. 'Don't, Paul! That's what hell is, for me : the place without light where I am lost, lost, and all the rest of the world is lost and wandering too!'

He liked to torture her so that afterwards he could give her comfort. She had made him sadistic. When she said that they were bad for each other, she spoke the truth.

'You're strange,' Anne pondered, recovering. 'An agnostic, yet you read the Bible very often, don't you?'

His mouth tautened in the ironical expression she well knew. 'As philosophy. The old philosophers, the old mythologists, said with such ease all that the modern ones flounder about trying, without the elegance of conviction, to repeat. It was

185

the Bible,' he affirmed, 'that made me an agnostic. I've rarely met the arguments for non-belief put more lucidly than in the Book of Job.'

'You too, you're not happy. Why are intelligent people never happy?' she asked.

'None of us is the kind to be satisfied with the next best, if we can't attain the best. We'd rather admit we've failed.'

'Failed, *so far!*' she said with vigour. 'I think I'll die trying to clutch whatever it is that's escaped me all my life.'

They had come, again, close; very gently, experimentally, their lips touched, stayed a few seconds together, and withdrew.

'So very dear to me . . .' she said, and sighed, as she recognised the cadences of elegy.

'Anne?'

'Paul?' she said, seeking to turn their rising desire into jest. 'Come.'

As though in apology, 'If only there was some concert,' she cried, 'between the mind and . . .' (she gestured downwards) 'this!'

'Isn't there, then? It doesn't matter. Come.'

Janice

And since even in Paradise itself, the tree of knowledge was placed in the middle of the garden, whatever was the ambient figure, there wanted not a centre and rule of decussation.

Sir Thomas Browne, *The Garden of Cyrus*

Janice

1

When Paul and I lay clasped and dying, what each of us did, and what we did together, involved in its intentions us two alone. Roddy was not in the bed; nor Celia; Kiri was not in the bed, nor Alan nor Janice nor any of her friends. There were temporarily no ghosts. In this respite from silences, even if at all other times the secret, unmentioned part of our separate existences loomed larger and loomed large, we did not cheat, did not cozen, did not lie.

As the months passed, I realised that thought of Roddy and Celia could be switched off whenever they themselves were absent. What could not, for me, be switched off was thought of Janice. What could not be switched off was guilt.

Guilt was sufficiently common. I tended to diagnose as guilt every pain not dealt with by the dentist. Where Paul would have taken an aspirin, where Celia lit a candle, I, swigging whisky, said to myself, 'Guilt,' and, when I had wiped my mouth, usually found work to be the palliative.

There were, however, times when work seemed impossible.

To assume, as for so long I did, that I knew the reason, was not wise, for the mind may outwit its owner. When, finally, our quarrels revealed to me that I was attempting to shift to Paul the blame for my uneasiness, I began to see that the true cause of the feeling was not the dead child. The dead child invariably came to mind when I could not work; but the dead child was associated with other dead children : was associated with Paul's wife, whose love of children was famous—and who put no children in her books.

As I was considering whether it would be entirely fantastical, seem flippant, seem callous, to pay her a visit in order to clarify our relations (I had an urge, defiant and yet deep, to hear myself called a rotten little whore), I received, to my surprise, a card requesting my attendance at her house. The purpose of the invitation she left undisclosed. Saying nothing to Paul, I conveyed to her my acceptance, and one afternoon the following week, in the capricious weather of early autumn, late summer, set off.

A pleasant housekeeperish woman admitted me. The house was vast—vaster, I soon recognised, than it looked from outside, and from outside it was not small. Upstairs, I was left to wait for a few minutes in a kind of antechamber; then nods and smiles indicated that I might go in, and the woman withdrew.

The moss-coloured carpet was so thick that I was conscious of very little but the soft, silent, pleasurable way my feet sank into it as I crossed to the main door. Recording the design of the handle, curiously elaborate, on my fingers rather than with my eyes, I pushed, and the door swung unexpectedly wide, leaving me to confront, as it flashed back, broken glimpses of avenues, fountains, cypress trees, and, with such a shock that I very nearly cried out, my own face.

Completely unnerved, I found the landscape was no longer there. A husky voice intoned :

        ' "Ere Babylon was dust,
  The Magus Zoroaster, my dead child,
  Met his own image, walking in the garden.
  That apparition, sole of men, he saw." '

Then the word 'image' registered. I stood, my heart still noisily thudding, before one of very many mirrors.

'Not that that is true, in one sense,' said Janice, propped with apparent comfort against a mound of pillows in her huge bed. 'The *Doppelgänger* phenomenon seems to be common enough, especially with the mystics and other schizophrenes.' She grinned at me, 'The Egyptians thought we all had one— "ka", they called it, a sort of identical twin. Disturbing, though, to meet it, just like that. Poor girl! Come and sit down. People,' she added, 'have seen some very strange things in gardens.'

I moved, and the image in the mirror before me also moved.

'Come,' she said impatiently. 'I don't like to ask people twice to do the same thing.'

Obediently I crossed to a chair. She treated me rather as I treated men; for our frustrations she penalised the healthy, I the male.

There were mirrors all round the room, but the effect was not vulgar. It was, on the contrary, light and fluent, with a swift elegance and a wit. In the colours: white, gold, amber, pink; the asymmetrical, curvilinear patterns; the rhythms, rocking, swaying; the whole bitter-sweet, laughing, melancholy mood, she had caught the spirit of rococo to perfection. Too mocking to be called voluptuous, too flirtatious to be sensual, too wistful to be gay, it was like her books: slender, haunting, an appeal for backward glances, a love-affair with illusion. On one wall was a little Fragonard. I only missed the minuets and the opera, and a pile of gramophone records topped by a mask and a fan showed that even that lack had already been supplied.

'Zoroaster,' I said. 'I don't know much about him.'

'None of your half-truths, child! If you're like the rest of your generation, you don't know anything about him at all. Or about anything else, for that matter.'

'I know about Zoroaster that in the wilderness he lived on cheese for twenty years. You'll find I don't tell lies. And I'm not like the rest of my generation,' I said.

'No, you're not,' she retorted. 'I give you that. Your faults are bigger, one can tell it from your work. Well, what else do you know about him?'

'Zoroaster? Only the essentials: that he founded the religion of Old Persia and the Parsees, and is also called Zarathustra.'

'Not much, is it?' she said triumphantly. 'What can you tell me about Ormuzd and Ahriman, nothing?'

'Only that Ormuzd, the good principle, wins in the end,' I responded.

'You girls would have done far better to stay at home than go to school. I can't think what they taught any of you there.'

'Useless things.' I affirmed. 'The whole syllabus needs changing—in fact, there shouldn't be a syllabus. But Zoroastrianism —you've studied that too?'

'You mean Babylon is supposed to be my subject, apart from the fictions. You *are* like the rest of your generation; you think everybody ought to be allowed one subject, or one piece of a subject, and never stray outside.'

'I think nothing of the kind.'

'Good. I'm glad to hear it. Well, all religions are interesting, don't you agree? But Babylonia I found especially . . . what shall I say—picturesque? Mainly it's the sculpture— cylindrical sculpture, whereas almost every other nation on earth chipped at damned great blocks and rounds. And once they'd discovered how pretty lapis-lazuli eyes look on metal-work, the Babylonians still had the good sense to leave their statues blank. You wouldn't find that anywhere else. It all gets mixed up with Persia, of course, when Cyrus comes along. *I* first came to it the other way round, though, through Browne, as a matter of fact—you know, the *Garden of Cyrus* and things—as an incidental result of following up his theory that the number five has some sort of magical as well as aesthetic significance. The Hanging Gardens are his prime example. But I admire the way you manœuvre round to real, unimportant things,' she said with a smile. 'It would have been such a disappointment if when you'd eventually come you'd started talking about you and me and others in the case, with our immortal souls flung in, instead of honest-to-God trivialities.'

Not aware of having talked of anything very much, 'But you're a Catholic, aren't you?' I asked.

'Sort of. No divorce forthcoming. Sorry and all that, but you must just wait till I'm dead, which won't be long. Oh,' she added, 'I'm a Catholic only by habit. Everything else has very much lapsed. Intellectually, I'm a Taoist.'

'I'm afraid my education fails me once again.'

She laughed. 'It's simple. According to Chuang Chou, the idea is to be empty. "The perfect man's use of his mind is like a mirror. He does not anticipate events, nor does he go counter to them. Thus it is that he is able to master things and not be injured by them." '

'Mmm,' I responded. 'You mean if you do nothing you can absorb everything?'

'No,' she said sharply. 'I mean what I say!'

'You say what Chuang Chou meant, or said. And usually there's a disparity between one's own thoughts and someone else's style.'

'In other words, why am I not more original?'

'I had thought, by your own reasoning, there *were* no other words?'

She gurgled with laughter. 'It's not wise to be unkind to your examiner. But you pass, child, you pass. No, I read too much, and unfortunately I remember most of what I read; it impedes my own thought.'

'Untrue,' I commented. 'I've read some of your books. For a woman, you think and write very well.'

'And you paint very well, for a woman.'

We both laughed. 'Actually,' she added, 'I have one of your earliest things here—bought long before your name meant anything to me. A sketch. I don't usually like sketches, apart from those of Watteau; in fact, I don't much like yours, now. But then, your execution has changed, thank God, as much as my taste!'

'Heavens, it's such a long time since I did any drawing, except with the brush! Might I see it?'

She nodded. 'On the far wall, look!'

Roddy stared inexorably back at me.

'Oh, God!' I said, recoiling. After a while I returned to my chair. Janice was watching me and deliberately noting every reaction.

'May I buy it from you?' I asked, not meeting her eyes.

'Poor child!' she said briskly. 'Poor poor child! No, it wouldn't be wise of you to take it, till I'm dead and you can all do as you like. Would it? If you really wanted, I'd give it to you, but you know it would make the hurt worse, surely?'

I was silent.

'His son's very much like him, isn't he?' she remarked, with the same deliberation.

'His *son*?'

She nodded emphatically.

I went back to the picture.

She was quite right. The sketch was of Stephen: an imaginary Stephen, a schoolgirl's pin-up Stephen, Stephen conceived as, if he had been less clever, he might have seemed at the age of twenty or twenty-five. I stood regarding it, remembering now with the utmost clarity the day that I had found it was missing: the searching everywhere without knowing why it mattered so much; the continued failure of the search. For a few seconds the ache stayed with me; then it was gone, and there was nothing. When I thought of Roddy, when I thought of Stephen, there was nothing, except confusion and relief.

Returning accusingly to Janice, 'How did *you* come to possess it?' I asked.

'I bought it.'

'*Yes*, but—from Stephen?'

'From Roddy,' she said.

Musical instruments had always been expensive.

She plucked a fallen rose-petal from the table by the bed, and handed it to me. Still thinking, I raised it absently to my nostrils.

She became curt. 'Throw it away! It's dead. Don't be a sentimental fool. What did you think that stupid boy would give you? Love? Happiness?'

'Yes,' I said defiantly. 'Both those things. And he's not stupid.' But it was hardly worth bothering about; I had begun to feel her judgement was apt.

'Immature, then. You should know better, at your age. Don't people read Herbert Spencer any more? If they did, you'd have discovered by now that no one can be free, or moral, or happy, till everyone is happy and moral and free.'

'So we just wait here for the human race to perfect itself?' I said furiously, 'How long do you imagine that little job will take?'

'There's no harm in beginning to perfect yourself meanwhile. But at some time or other you'll have to learn to wait, and a good way of spending the interval is to assist the process of perfection in other people.'

'I hate and despise perfection! What has perfection to do with freedom or morality or happiness?'

'Quite a lot, hasn't it?' Janice replied. 'Why is it you think you have a right to be happy?'

'Oh, I *don't*! I only claim the right to go on insisting that at present I'm not happy and that I'm not prepared to pretend I am.'

'I wonder, though,' Janice said thoughtfully, 'why you say it as if you really mean you're going through hell on earth, and as if—which is worse—you want to make everyone agree you are, and swear they are too?'

'Do you think we can ever get closer to hell than this?'

'Maybe this is also the closest we shall ever be to heaven. And if that is so,' she observed, 'what we decide to call our particular state, whether hell, or heaven, or purgatory, is a serious matter, since it may decide the nomenclature of that state for all eternity.'

Angered, I said nothing.

'Why are you so preoccupied with happiness?' she demanded.

'I'm not!'

'But you *are*! Why don't you think about good instead? Or evil, since the one implies the other?'

'Because,' I said, 'whenever I'm good I'm acutely miserable, and evil frightens me.'

'You're miserable when you think you're good. But you've stopped being good the moment you're conscious of virtue.'

'Well—I *want* to be good—isn't wanting to be good itself a sign of virtue?'

'Nonsense, child! You don't want to be good. You only want to stop feeling physical desire, because of the trouble it involves you in. Or you want to be happy, and you're terribly afraid that goodness is the only means to your end.'

'That of course is perfectly true.'

'But when you're working you're happy, aren't you?'

'Am I? I never think about it then.'

·That the first requisite for happiness: unconsciousness.

'Like Celia?' I said gloomily.

'No—not, at least, like Celia as she *was*. You have to have been conscious, first, of happiness.'

As I had feared, I was in moderation liking her, and distrusting her immensely. This middle-aged woman, who was contemporary with Stephen; who had been the wife of Paul; who had, it now appeared, conducted negotiations, and dubious ones, with the youthful Roddy, figured in rumours of which I should have preferred not to think.

The silence intensified. I believe she guessed the cause. As the atmosphere underwent a subtle alteration, I caught sight of a vista in one of the mirrors that made me cross over to the opposite window and gaze curiously down on the gardens that stretched beneath.

Janice looked at me. Her eyes held an expression I had never seen in a woman before—intimate and conspiring. I felt uncomfortable, yet at the same time attracted. If it had been a man, I should have been certain the attraction was physical and there would have been no need for discomfort.

'By the way,' she said, 'was it afterwards, or in Guatemala, that Celia became Paul's mistress?'

2

It was another season, outside. Outside, it was winter. Along the broad avenues, the interminable walks where soundless cypresses stood, no flowers were visible. No flower would ever be visible, and it would always be winter, in the garden outside. From the oval pond in the centre, where the largest of the fountains was placed, every walk was the same walk: lugubrious, cold, deserted, leading past the same columns, the same fountains, the same soundless cypresses, away, immense, into the distance, through great masses of trees.

'... Paul's mistress?'

Rigid, frozen, the hedges might be made of stone. The fountains were frozen, with their leaden urns; their water, streaming, was always the same water; glacial, it did not move. The cascades were the same cascades.

'... Paul's mistress?'

The pools reflected the same buildings, the same mirrors; the same mirrors reflected the same pools, the same fountains, the same soundless cypresses and the hedges that might be made of stone: a labyrinth, the same labyrinth, where there were no flowers and where the walks led to the same oval in the same centre, making the shape of the garden, framed by great masses of trees, quincuncial, a comment on the magical and the aesthetic significance of the number five. The basins, reflecting the buildings and the tall clipped hedges, the marble columns and the river gods, the groups of playing children sculpted beside the leaden urns that served to ornament the ornamental fountains, were reflected themselves in the child-less mirrors, chill voluptuousness of stone.

'... or in Guatemala, Paul's mistress?'

I turned, 'Is it as clear as that, would you think?' I asked. 'I've never even really understood why he went there.'

'Oh,' she said, 'he went there because I sent him, but I don't suppose he realises that.'

I studied her face. She glanced (she had already glanced several times) at her silver wrist-watch. and blandly turned on the wireless by the bed.

'Just as,' a replica of her throaty voice declaimed, 'the countryside of Norfolk is filled for us now with the golden light that for Constable had always been there, and just as Arles writhes before us as it writhed before Van Gogh—rich field for a cry of carrion crows—so it is no longer possible, after seeing a picture by Anne Rivers, to look upon a Jamaican face without beholding it through her eyes: through the clear warm passionate eyes of love.'

We listened to silence for a moment; then, frowning, Janice held her watch up to her ear, muttering something about a concert, and rapidly manipulated the knob of the wireless-set till there was a click.

She might be a very clever woman—only a clever woman would possess a baroque garden and a rococo bedroom—but she would have done well to remember that I was not entirely stupid. Her watch said exactly the same as mine, and mine had not stopped.

'Don't you see it looking back at you with hate?' I asked.

'One can learn to accept that hate, and not to shrink away.'

I made no answer.

'Anne, my dear!' she said softly. 'As you have already learned.'

Even though I knew it was what she wanted me to do, I stood up, restless, and, shaking my head impatiently, moved away.

'What is it?' she asked.

'Life,' I said. 'Every damned thing in the world.'

'You loved your Jamaican very much?'

'People seldom ask me, even mentally, that question.'

'I'm impertinent, you mean?'

'The questions people *do* usually put are the impertinence —they're all based on the assumption that it must have been —surely?—nothing but sex. With, not far off, the unspoken belief that niggers stink. Stink of sex. Because, when people say the Negro stinks, they mean only that he doesn't have to undress to prove his manhood. And why that should be a crime if it were true I'll never understand.'

'Their attitude is reasonable, in this case,' she remarked. 'You paint your Negro lecherous.'

'He was a lecher, "my" Jamaican. He was black. I didn't love the lechery, and to the blackness I was indifferent. But the whole of him I loved, yes, very much.'

'Then what's the problem?'

It was growing dark, and before I answered she requested me to put on the lights.

'Only,' I said, regaining my chair, 'that I'm beginning not to love him any more. It took four years to forget his face, and five to . . . In another two I shall have forgotten his hands, and at the end of nine, ten years, love. Love, a word I don't even like to use, because I know its meaning so well. That's the problem: that you can love across the seas and up to the sky, higher than Everest—love inexplicably—and it still takes only ten years, to forget. One didn't ask, one doesn't want, to be as shallow as one has been created.'

'You painted lechery because you're obsessed with a desire to be chaste. Even if, like Augustine, "not yet". But you will never be chaste till you love again.'

'I love all the time. Six men at once, all the bloody time!'

'You've never loved but once in your life, and then by mistake. You use your mind too much.'

But I was thinking now of the pictures. 'I should have liked to combine the vision of Piero della Francesca and Van Gogh. . . .'

'Heavens, child! Isn't it enough for you that Piero went blind and the Dutchman mad? Must you do both? Anyway, you could never be a Piero! Don't you realise that none of your thought registers in your paintings? That it's so much wasted time? If you wish to think in paint, you must lighten your palette, make it as light as that of Piero himself—and if you lighten your palette you must be a man! Otherwise, all the critics will say in glee, "How pretty!" and you will become an R.A., the painter in you crucified alive!'

This attitude in her surprised me. 'Does being a woman make you so bitter, Janice?'

She hesitated, for the first and almost the only time in our acquaintance. 'I'm too old for bitterness, and not a woman any more. But I would like the English to accept, one day, both that to be a female is not a major sin, and, simultaneously, that a female writer would rather be called a worse Stendhal than a better Elizabeth Barrett or George Sand. And not the English only—even in France . . . For instance, Simone de Beauvoir has written one of the best political novels of all time in *Les Mandarins*, better than anything of Sartre, but does anyone treat it as that?'

'You do,' I observed.

'I? I'm a woman—I don't count!'

I laughed. 'It's always possible that if a woman goes on saying a thing long enough, a man may repeat it as his own, and then its importance will be acknowledged.'

In the bright lights she looked all at once very old. 'Ring for the housekeeper,' she ordered. 'It's time for my medicine, and you must go, before you wear me out with your feministic nonsense.'

Propped against the pillows, her little face still as vivacious as a monkey's, an old, old monkey's, she began to comb out her fringe with her fingers, and when I had obediently pushed the bell and said goodbye, she muttered perfunctorily, 'You don't count either, but come back some time, I want to talk to you again. Come back tomorrow afternoon.'

*

Turning the corner sharply as I came from the antechamber, and, as usual, looking in the opposite direction from the one in which I was going since, as usual, my bearings were lost, I collided with a girl.

'Sorry.'

'My fault,' I replied.

It was the girl who had gate-crashed our party. We stood regarding each other fixedly, with a number of unsaid things troubling the air. She, however, had the advantage, since her strategy was the aggressor's, and I did not yet know for certain what I was supposed to be defending.

'The staircase . . .?' I asked.

She pointed, and moved on. I had a ridiculous feeling that somehow, even in asking her the way, I had left myself unguarded; and I did not like to look back, in case she should still be watching me.

*

When I arrived the next afternoon we passed each other again. This time she was engaged in a conversation—almost, it seem an argument—with Celia, who was so intent on whatever they were discussing that she did not notice my approach, though the girl herself gave me a familiar nod.

' 'lo, Celia,' I said.

'Oh—hallo, Anne!' She smiled.

I went again over the thick soft pleasurable carpet that children would have made so dirty, into the room of mirrors, where Janice was huddled over a tray containing writing materials and did not look up at my entry. Perhaps, I thought, she had not heard my knock. The array of silver pens and pencils, virginal blotters, white luxurious paper, gleaming ink-wells, amused me; I was reminded of the ritualistic preparations of the Chinese calligrapher in times gone by, adding musk, and powdered jade, to his inks, to dignify and placate them.

I coughed.

Still scribbling, she spoke. 'Yes, I know you're there.'

'In that case, may I sit down?'

'Your pictures aren't exactly comfortable to have on one's walls.'

'Then,' I said wearily, sitting, 'how do you suppose it feels to live with them in one's mind?'

Glancing up, 'You don't after all *want* to have back your sketch of—you don't *want* your sketch?' she asked.

I shook my head. 'Who's the girl I met talking with Celia in the corridor?'

'My secretary, probably. At least, that's how she's officially described.'

Several interpretations of this remark occurred to me. Head supported on hand, Janice maliciously watched my face, and said, 'She's here, I mean, to await my death. Much like the rest of you.'

Embarrassed, I demurred, but she would not hear out my objection.

'Whether it's by accident or design, and whether I can help it, makes no difference—I'm in the way of all of you, and when I'm dead there'll be nothing but your stupidities to prevent you from marrying Roddy, or Celia from marrying Paul.'

Argument was evidently useless. 'In what sense is the girl waiting for your death?' I inquired.

'Among other things, she's expecting a reward for services rendered. But also she doesn't like me very much. Jasmine Donald's her name—an old enemy of yours, I believe.'

'So *that's* who she is?' But I was still puzzled. 'It's so odd, the way she keeps popping up in unexpected places. . . .'

'Only if you assume it happens by chance. If I were you I'd work out what her game is, and devise a counterploy. It shouldn't be hard, she's not all that intelligent, but I think she sees you as a kind of rival.'

'But why should she? What reason has she to involve herself in my life?'

Janice reflected. 'Perhaps at some time you wandered across her own little strip? I'd say it was originally a simple case of "I do not love thee, Dr Fell".' She paused. 'And then, of course, she's Roddy's present mistress.'

Used by now to her lobbing of bomb-shells, I showed little reaction. 'I wondered about that when we first met.'

'And you dismissed the idea? Yes, the thing dates from fairly recently, I'd say. But her main object's money, not sex.' She picked up a wad of manuscript, and seemed to be about to make some remark concerning it, but after running her gaze over a few pages she changed her mind. The movement introduced a new subject, nevertheless.

'You're writing another book?' I asked.

'Why, do you think my writing life is already finished? No, I mustn't tease you.' She flicked the papers with her fore-finger and thumb. 'This is a children's book, a little fairy-tale called *The Good King's Daughter*, that I'm doing to keep my hand in while the ideas for bigger things are forming. At present I'm stuck in my *magnum opus*. I thought I had it here,' she said parenthetically, 'but apparently not. When the first draft's finished I'd rather like to have your opinion of it.'

Despite the casualness of the tone, she did not meet my eyes as she said 'my *magnum opus*'.

'You pay me a great compliment,' I answered, 'but my opinion on things literary wouldn't be professional enough to be of much benefit to you.'

'I don't want any comment on its style. What I'm concerned with is its truth,' she immediately responded.

'Oh, truth!' I scoffed.

'Yes, truth. I want to know whether my book seems to you a fair representation of the facts about people . . . people you will find are familiar.'

'It's not a novel, then?' I questioned.

'Yes, in form it's fictional . . .'

'But you want to know whether it seems real? I'm not sure there's any profitable distinction to be made between reality and illusion—your fancies are as good or bad as mine, so why do you need my views on the validity of your visions?'

'You'll find you're implicated, in a way,' she replied.

'Then my testimony is suspect.'

'I can trust you to tell me what is true,' she stated with immense conviction.

'What was it Congreve said: "No mask like open truth to cover lies"?'

'About my work, that's as may be; but you won't lie to me, Anne.'

'I'd better tell you, at least,' I remarked, my tone light and frivolous, 'I'm most terribly jealous of you.'

'No matter, child, and that I had already sensed. What you forget is that I may feel the same of you.'

'You love Paul still?' I asked awkwardly, abandoning the pretence of facetiousness.

She put her head on one side, as if considering whether to answer this or some related question. 'You ought to know,' she said, 'love doesn't stop just because it has every reason to.'

'All the same . . .'

'Oh,' she interrupted, 'it was certainly I who sent him packing! But who takes the initiative in recognising the end has come is really so irrelevant, in marriage or an affair. We'd both known for a long time it was all over bar the elegies. I had realised, you see, that it wasn't the male in him that attracted me, but the female. And that frightened me; I was repelled.' She became impatient with herself. 'As though even an apparently unambiguous choice, like that of the paederast, disguises anyone's bisexuality! As though there were no Lesbians who love the male in their female mates!' Tapping them together, she fastened her papers up. 'But then Paul became aware of what I'd discovered, which was unfortunately something of which he had always been afraid. He sees so much more than he comments on, Anne, don't let his dryness deceive you.'

'Yes,' I said.

'Of course, you're his mistress, you'd be clearer-sighted than I!'

I shifted uncomfortably.

'Ah, I wasn't jabbing at you! How you young people flinch at words!' She gave her raucous throaty laugh. 'How absurd you are, the young! How lovable, and completely absurd! You think, because I'm an old woman, I must imagine all mistresses are wicked, and all wives the incarnation of virtue? You think I haven't been the mistress of a married man? You think I don't know what it is like to see pictures of the wedding? Of the bride? You resent my mirrors, but remember what I've spared you! I've spared you the photographs. Or have you seen them somewhere else, Anne, my poor child?'

'Paul has a few pictures of you,' I replied, somewhat sourly.

I preferred her when she was *not* playing the famous novelist of French extraction.

'Ah, he has?' She seemed more startled than pleased at first, but then the slow, almost fatuous grin of flattered vanity apppeared a moment on her face, bringing to my own, though she shook a warning finger at me, a smile she observed without resentment. Then she said, with no change of tone, 'Draw the curtains. It hasn't occurred to you that I might have liked to stake a claim in Roddy?'

Doing as she bade, I shut out with two quick gestures the frozen gardens, and crossed the cool, vibrantly feminine little room back to my chair. 'As a matter of fact,' I said, 'it has. And that you tried to stake it long ago, by marrying Paul, who you thought had been his lover.'

3

We developed the habit of almost daily discussing in her room the various subjects that interested us. In my fondness for her astringent society I came nearly to forget how soon she would be dead, and to forget also how hard she worked whenever I wasn't there. It was a surprise when one day she presented to me the manuscript, renewing her demand that I should give her my opinion of it.

'I've already told you there must be better judges of its literary worth. And about its truth,' I pleaded, 'I can only guess.'

' "To read" originally *meant* "to guess".' She sighed. 'I wonder what "to write" meant?'

Obstinate, I continued to sit in my usual chair. She impatiently ordered me to be off. 'If you leave the book behind I shall send Jasmine after you with it; and I don't want to see you again until you've finished!'

Within a few minutes of me, Paul too arrived home. We had seen little of each other in the last few days, and his aloof manner struck me now as odd. Nothing happened to explain it until we had eaten, when he asked suddenly, 'Why didn't you mention that you were meeting Janice?'

At his hostile tone my defences immediately went up. 'There seemed no reason why I should.'

'Common courtesy ought to have provided at least one!'

'Good heavens, Paul, you're pompous lately! Do you expect to be informed of every visit made to your wife? You're separated from her, after all!'

'That's not the point,' he angrily retorted. 'I'm not separated from *you*!'

'A simple explanation of *that* might be that you've never been married to me!'

'You mean if we did marry you wouldn't expect the thing to last?'

'What *does* last? I don't think we'd better go into such dubious hypotheses at present. I only wanted to remind you that the chains certainly haven't been fastened on me yet. You're mistaken if you imagine you can exact duties from someone to whom you've so far granted no privileges.'

'You don't want to marry me, do you?' His voice expressed doubt, momentary humility; what answer he desired was to me by no means clear.

'Is it Leap Year or something, that you're waiting for proposals? I *won't* be treated as anybody's chattel! I've never questioned you about your own movements; I've a right to the same liberty myself. It isn't that I've deliberately concealed anything from you; I had no idea you'd be particularly interested.'

He looked disbelieving.

Still slightly on the defensive, 'Who told you about it?' I asked.

'That's none of your business.'

'If you've been having me spied on, it's very much my business to find out the cause. What is it that I'm being accused of, and by whom?'

'Is there something you could be accused of, then? What

reason have you for not wishing what you do when I'm out to be known?'

'I think I have a perfect right to resent my freedom's being infringed, and I object intensely to the idea of espionage.'

We glared at each other, and I burst out laughing. 'We're both being absurd! What is it—has someone been sending you anonymous letters?'

'No—don't be silly. Of course I trust you, and no one's been playing the detective. I was just . . . well, rather hurt, that's all. Janice's secretary let it slip out that you'd been visiting the house. It was a bit embarrassing; she must have realised from my reaction that I didn't know.'

' "Let it slip out",' I mocked. 'I can imagine how easily that happened!'

'What do you mean? She seems to me a very nice girl.'

'She doesn't seem in the least like that to me. By the way, Paul, did you know she's Roddy's mistress?'

'I don't believe it,' he said.

'That's what Janice told me, anyway. I think it's very likely to be true.'

'Janice! She's nothing left to do but gossip,' he said with heat and some scorn.

'She still writes. And she can hardly help being confined to bed. Incidentally,' I remarked, 'when have you ever told me that *you* visit her?'

'That I visit her? But I—oh,' he said, 'I see. I—I thought I had.'

'We won't quarrel over it,' I replied, watching him carefully.

Apparently about to speak, he changed his mind, lighting a cigarette instead.

'Paul,' I said, 'would you please tell me how Miss Donald came to make her revelation that I visit Janice?'

He seemed uncomfortable. 'We happened somehow to have got on to the subject of her will. The girl is anxious that Janice should be protected from . . . well, from . . .'

'Fortune-hunters?' I asked. 'She just happened to introduce my name in that context; and she just happened to be passing this house? Because you didn't meet her at your wife's at all, did you?'

He would not meet my eyes. 'There's no need to be unduly sensitive, or so suspicious, Anne. I'm sure she didn't mean to imply anything unpleasant.'

'I understand. It's just that my name and the mention of fortune-hunters somehow happened to be juxtaposed!'

'Anne . . .'

'One moment. There's something to say. Janice hasn't any other surviving relations, has she?'

'No,' he said.

'Wouldn't you agree, then, that the likeliest candidates for what she may leave are you, Celia, Roddy, and—Miss Donald herself?'

He flushed. 'I think that's pretty despicable. You're really behaving as if you were jealous of the girl.'

'And you're behaving as if you're sweet on the girl. You probably don't realise, though, that she and I have already met, and I have every reason for nursing a grudge.'

'Yes, she's told me that,' he replied. 'I don't think any previous misunderstanding should make you launch blind attacks on her now.'

'There was no misunderstanding, and no one is launching any blind attacks. What *has* the girl been saying to you about me?'

'She's only been defending Janice's interests.' He looked away again. 'I merely want to point out that the likeliest candidate, as you put it, for my wife's money is, at the present moment, yourself, and out of us all you are hardly the person who is most in need of it.'

'Wait a minute,' I said. 'Not only am I not in need of being left Janice's money, I am also profoundly uninterested in receiving it. Nor, if you'll only *think*, does Celia want or need it. Your rivals, Paul my dear, are Roddy and Miss Donald, and if I were you I'd consider the possibility that they might have formed a combination. The only other thing I feel like saying,' I added, 'is that I find this subject sordid in the extreme.'

He went a darker red. 'People who have money always do find the discussion of it sordid! But if you could bear condescending, all the same, to . . .'

'I worked for what money I have, and I'm not, as you seem to be suggesting, a millionaire!'

'Other people work just as hard as you.'

'You'll forgive me if I say that I respect achievement more than effort. And using such a criterion . . .'

'You wouldn't put me among the people who work as hard as you!' he completed angrily.

'I haven't said that, and I didn't mean to imply it.'

I would have continued, but just then we both noticed the time shown on the clock, and with an exclamation he began to gather up the material for his next lecture.

*

When Paul had gone I settled down, reluctantly, with the manuscript of the novel that was to be Janice's last, and, many people say, her best.

Perhaps, in literature, it was the equivalent of the landscape which she had created outside her windows. It may also have been her own quizzical exploration of the number that had fascinated her favourite author: the number five; for the characters were five, and five the parts of the book, one for each. We were all portrayed there, Celia, Roddy, Paul, Janice herself, and I—styled only by our initials, as if in one of the contemporary French novels she so much liked to criticise and parody and read. It was also the story of a love, her love for my guardian, for Roddy's and Celia's father, her love for Stephen, whom she never named, who never appeared except through other people's eyes, who was for her one of the darker gods, and with whom died her faith. It was the story of a life and of a love that she herself would probably have called *perdu*.

I skimmed on till I reached the scene in which J gives the manuscript of her would-be *magnum opus*, her final, and most complex, work, to the reluctant A in order to obtain her judgement of it.

The maze, the Chinese puzzle, the Russian doll, the corridor of mirrors, every similar artifice, may from the outside be interesting in the extreme; it is frightening, from within. Flicking hastily over the next few pages, where A begins to read the novel (prefaced with a quotation from Browne) in which her *alter ego* is asked for an opinion of the manuscript that is its author's ultimate and major work, I came to the passage wherein are set forth the provisions of J's last will and testament, by whose means, it slowly became clear to me, she sought to release us from our present bonds—and impose on us new ones of her own.

With a sick feeling I set down the manuscript. It was clever, her solution. Her every move was clever, and a mistake. The flaw in her reasoning was always the same: to suppose that the sum of the parts equals only the whole. Thus, by showing me the study of Stephen I had made when a schoolgirl, she revealed to me that Roddy was no more than the incidental paradigm of an older, more comprehensive love; but, having discovered that, she had not seen the conclusions to which it led. Again, she recognised the menace represented by Jasmine, yet gave her no part in the plot. She surrounded herself with mirrors, to catch the fleeting expression, the unguarded look; she failed, however, to realise that in those same mirrors her guests might come to a full awareness of her and of themselves. She failed, in addition, to realise that in mirrors of my own I had already made, for better or for worse, my choice. She could not indeed be expected to know it; for she had not attended our party.

*

Celia often teased me about our taste in furniture. Both Paul and I liked, above all, comfort, and the feeling of comfort was given us best by ample arm-chairs, huge tables and sideboards; mellow browns shading through rust and copper; thick rugs; the soft play of light.

'Confess, now,' she used to tell me, 'if you saw all this in someone else's house, the famous eyebrow would immediately shoot up and you would murmur, "How very, very wholesome!"'

'On the contrary, one always tends to be lenient to one's favourite vice,' I replied.

'In oneself, that may be. Not, I've noticed, in other people!'

The room was by now so familiar that normally I did not see it at all. At the party, however, it became, as a familiar room suddenly will when invaded by guests, different, alien.

Over the sideboard and the chimney-piece were mirrors, multiplying the ample arm-chairs, enhancing the soft play of light. Yet all at once they encouraged queer clashes, queer strenuous conflicts, of harsh reality and harsher illusion. I was reminded, then, of the painting in which Manet shows the barmaid at the Folies-Bergère, first frontally, and then, to her own right, reflected, at a diagonal, in the glass behind her, apparently busying herself with a customer. But *is* she busy with, is she talking to, a customer? Her face is foolish, vacant, dreamy, her thoughts, melancholy, are far away; she is looking slightly downward, as if for the moment unoccupied. Yet in the glass behind her—her hair-style changed?—she looks up, into the intent eyes of a stranger, the eyes of a shabby, pleading, mustachioed Satan who might to her be the very embodiment of the respectable. In their silent *tête-à-tête* the chatter of the fashionable *demi-monde* around them disappears, and, with the glinting bottles, the tangerines, the roses, the noise, the blaze of light from the chandeliers above them forgotten, they are completely alone, lost girl and bulbous-nosed man.

In like manner our room that night was filled with segregated, sequestered couples seen first frontally, then reflected diagonally to infinity in manifold, multiple, multitudinous mirrors: Celia and I, Celia and Roddy, Paul and Celia, Paul and I. There were times when I wanted to give a wild scream of laughter, when I expected all of us to be converted into cut-glass decanters, tastefully garnished, but at those moments someone was always at my elbow, solicitous, and as the night wore on it seemed to me that the solicitous person at my elbow who would not let me alone was always and invariably Paul: offering me punch, offering me brandy, offering me vodka or rum or whisky with lime-juice, offering at last to take me upstairs and put all my problems quietly, skilfully, masterfully to sleep.

But before then everything had become most annoyingly confused. I started to point out to the solicitous person at my elbow, who kept eccentrically turning into two solicitous persons, one at each elbow, with an improper number of eyes, that the way everyone, even people I had thought of as my friends, seemed to be finding it necessary to shout at each other was really quite inconsiderate. If, I was going to ask, they were deaf, why had they not brought their hearing-aids with them? Or, if that presented difficulties, why had not a few of them at least brought their hearing-aids, to share with the rest? Just then, however, I was afflicted, acutely, by the thought that 'hearing-aid' might not be a decent word. Did it, indeed, exist? And if it did exist, which in view of the room's tendency, hardly considerate again, to lurch and bounce and sway, seemed insusceptible of proof, was that—was that—? ? ?—and again, supposing—? ? ? But the solicitous person at one's elbow (surely one had once had *two* elbows?) who had just both unaccountably and discourteously withdrawn, taking, God forgive him, one's glass, was offering, or had offered, at the moment when one was least sure of his exist-ence, punch, or brandy, or vodka, or perhaps all of them, with soda, which was a very much less attractive idea (pos-sibly treasonable, as well as nauseous) than lime.

I appeared to be signalling. Stephen once taught me sema-phore, and I have never been able to forget.

'Darling, I was coming, you needn't have worried!'

'Paul?'

But somehow we were not, as I had imagined when we began to kiss, downstairs: we were in the bedroom, though even there we could not escape from the mirrors or, reflected in them, Celia and Roddy.

'Don't you see why I killed the baby?' I asked myself, per-haps out loud, my feet straying backwards and forwards, or sideways, in loops, in ribbons, in circles. 'It must have been revenge. It was because he didn't love me as much as I loved him and anyway I *didn't* love him—it was you, you all the time, it was you!'

'That's all right, sweetest, that's all right.' Lovely how the light touched the curve of his brow, my lips the curve of his mouth his 'Only,' I added, concentrating hard, 'we hadn't met then' mou-ou-outh.

Wobbling slightly as (also wobbling) he released me, I said, 'Oh my God, what are all those serpents doing here?'

'Serpents?' He seemed surprised. Perhaps he was a trifle drunk, but if he was I bountifully and resplendently forgave him. 'Darling, there isn't even one serpent here!'

He had always told me only the part of the truth he thought I could bear. Resplendently, bountifully, I forgave him that too.

Then he was saying or I was saying something neither of us understood, about love and jealousy and happiness, and we moved farther into the silent dark room where the serpents lurked, with one of us asking, not very steadily, where happiness might be found, and the other answering, with equal unsteadiness, 'Don't you sometimes find it, darling, with me?'

4

Opening the door, 'Why, hullo,' I said, 'what brings *you* here? An unexpected delight indeed.'

'It's that awful girl!' Celia burst out.

'Come and sit down.' I led her through the hall. 'The abominable Miss Donald? One minute, and I'll make some coffee.'

'I won't have any, thank you very much.'

'Well, *I* want some! It's already on, nobody is allowed to deprive me of it, and to keep me company will be much more pleasant for you than waiting while I slurp!'

Afterwards, she told me the problem was blackmail.

'And what have you been doing to make yourself liable for blackmail?'

'It's not *exactly* me . . .' she responded.

'Who then—Roddy?'

'In a way. Yes.'

'Suppose,' I said, with all possible patience, 'you begin at the beginning?'

Flushing slightly, she obeyed. 'You see—oh, it's all terribly difficult—the girl, that awful girl, is Janice's and Stephen's daughter!'

'I had rather wondered, when I saw all of you together for the first time, at our party.'

She was shaken. 'Yes, I suppose if *I* can see the resemblance, other people . . .'

'Oh no, it wouldn't be obvious in the least to anyone who didn't know your family very well. And she's certainly very unlike Janice! But where does the blackmail come in?'

'As you already know, she's been . . . for all I know she may still be . . .'

I whistled. 'Roddy's mistress! Yes, they must be . . . what? Half-brother and half-sister? And that would still count as incest?'

'So,' she said, 'if she wanted to speak to the police . . .'

'Has she suggested any such thing?'

No reply came.

'You haven't your usual charitable opinion of her!'

Celia placed the empty cup on the table at her side.

I looked at her more sharply. 'That's not all, is it, though? Roddy's told her something that she could use . . .' I broke off. 'Don't give her any money,' I ordered, after rapid thought. 'Don't whatever you do give her any money. That would simply be admitting . . . I doubt anyway whether it would shut her up. Look: for the time being, just play her along. Tell her you believe she's very likely to acquire some money soon and you are unable, to your great regret, to lend her any yourself. She'll follow what it's all about. Tell her, too, but as if it's forced out of you, that I advised you to say this.'

'*Is* she likely to acquire some money?' Celia asked.

'As things are at present, yes. Unfortunately!'

'You know,' she suddenly exclaimed, 'I could stand anything except that—that damned *giggle* of hers!'

'Lord, Celia, *you* mustn't start diving off the deep end! You're supposed to be our model of serenity, remember? Funny, I hadn't noticed the giggle. . . . Will you have another cup of coffee?'

She arose. 'Thank you very much, no, Anne. I must be . . .'

'I didn't mean I wanted you to leave. How perverse the

English are! I meant, would you *like* another cup, since I'm anyway having another myself?'

With a laugh she shook her head. 'You're sweet to me, but really I must go.'

In the hall we both stopped. 'Have you any intention of ever going back to Guatemala?' I asked curiously.

'To the mission?' She hesitated. 'I don't know. Anne—I—I feel terrible...'

'So do I. Don't let's talk about it. What would be the use? Listen: about the blackmail; it's not Janice you're scared she'll tell? Because there's not much Janice doesn't already know!'

'No. It's not Janice.'

*

The wind jostled the haughty cypresses and shook the water of the fountains into aberrant gusts of silver. In the avenues, branches had been broken off and leaves strewn down by the force of the storm.

Glancing away from the windows at Janice, 'You'll have to tell your gardener to sweep the paths,' I said.

'I've already told him,' said Janice. 'Hasn't he started on it yet?'

'You've never done any of the gardening yourself?' I asked.

She wrinkled up her nose in distaste at the idea. 'I just play God.'

Turning, I looked down again into the stony garden where winter always reigned, where there would never be visible or tangible a flower. Grey, lugubrious, cold, deserted, the walks led away past columns of marble, past silver-spraying fountains, sombre cypresses, children that never moved, deities who never spoke, interminably into the distance and the great masses of trees.

Huffing on the glass, I drew, thoughtfully, the figure of a child.

'Not one of your better efforts!' said Janice.

'What?' I asked, coming over towards her.

She shook her head.

217

'People,' I observed, 'who play God are apt to burn their fingers in hell.'

'You're talking about the manuscript?'

'I'm talking about playing God.'

She corrected herself. 'It's possible I should really have said, "I interpret God." To play Him would, I agree, be a little rash.'

'More than a little, I should have thought.'

'You haven't,' she suggested, 'ever considered Emerson's remark, "God offers to every mind its choice between truth and repose"?'

'You're right. I haven't.'

'Anne,' she said cajolingly, 'if you were offered—as perhaps you already may have been—such a choice (a difficult choice, of course!), you would, as an artist, choose truth, wouldn't you?'

'It might depend,' I replied, 'whose was the repose that I was asked to reject.'

'You're quibbling.'

'No.'

'I think you would always choose truth.'

I shrugged.

'Anne—what did you think of it?'

'The manuscript?'

Anger had entered the elegant feminine room. 'Yes, the manuscript.'

'I'd rather not say.'

'Come, Anne! It was understood you would tell me!'

'By whom?'

She said impatiently, 'I don't think I've given you any cause for the note of animosity in your voice. If I have, I'm sorry. But please remember one thing, Anne: I've not much time to live.'

Sighing, 'I made no promises,' I reminded her. 'You're attempting to give me exactly the same choice that's offered by Emerson's God. But I don't think I like a God who offers choices of that kind.'

'Yet, if he's the only God there is ...'

'Janice, do I understand the position aright? Your will is as described in the book?'

218

'I'm sure,' she said, 'you'll realise I don't go in for absolute literalism. The details . . .'

'To hell with the details!' I replied. 'You're leaving your money to Roderick, provided that he marries me; and in his default, you're leaving it to whomsoever shall marry Paul?'

She said with a grin, 'You're perfectly correct. In other words, I've allowed you two bites at the same large rosy apple. You don't stand to lose, whatever your decision, and if you act as I should prefer, Roddy stands to gain as well.'

'Only, I happen to prefer apples sour, small and green! You make me so furious I could kill you! Don't you see it's impossible now that I should marry either of those men?'

'Oh, Anne!' For a second she looked quite taken aback, quite stricken. 'Money isn't something to despise, surely? I know you don't overvalue it, but that's the very reason I am fond of you, and want you to . . .'

'To be corrupted?' I asked. 'To be bought up and re-sold at a profit?'

Her twinkle had gradually become a dark glitter; in the mirrors her face was ugly. 'What excuse is there for taking this tone? I am sufficiently your senior to expect from you in this house the ordinary observances of courtesy, even if you accord them nowhere and to no one else! If you wish to ruin your life, very well; very well, marry neither Roderick nor my husband! Continue drinking—oh yes, I can smell the whisky on your breath! Do as you please, and good riddance to you. But I had never thought, when first I invited you here —you, the woman who was indulging in a wanton affair with . . .'

'Cut out the bluster,' I said, 'and listen to me. Isn't it true that this whole thing is fixed purely and simply to spite your daughter?'

She dropped the manuscript. 'What . . . ?'

'You heard. You know. You understand me perfectly. I said your daughter, and I mean the girl you've done your best to warp and hurt ever since she was born. And you've made a pretty good job of it, I grant you! Oh, I understand what your original motive was. After you'd practically made your reputation as a novelist out of being the childless wife who adored children, it would have been a little inconvenient for you to give public recognition to your bastard daughter, wouldn't it? Especially as you hated every child not made, like your statues, out of stone! Especially as you were between marriages at the time, and it would certainly have damaged Stephen's career. Thus far, it's hideous, what you did, but in a way one could sympathise. Friends talk. Relations talk. So you had her put, didn't you, your darling daughter, into a foundlings' home, into a place where you could be sure she would develop a Cockney accent that you could then proceed to loathe! For this was the other thing: you had to punish her. You were jealous; you were superstitious; and to you she was the visible symbol of your sin. She *was* your sin, and so she had to be punished, she had to be debased, she had to be despised.'

'She's stupid,' said Janice suddenly. 'That's what you don't see, she's stupid, through and through.'

'If you were right in what you say, is stupidity anyone's fault but God's? Granting, that is, for the moment, that there is a God and that He is omnipotent, et cetera, et cetera, ad nauseam, ad inf. . . . If you were *right*, is stupidity something to scorn? But listen to me, that girl isn't stupid! You think she's stupid because so far she hasn't yelped. But if anyone's been stupid, it's you; what your daughter's doing is biding her time, and she has a plan, a plot, that I think even you would consider ingenious.'

She stared at me with mingled contempt and disbelief.

'You said something interesting just now,' I went on. 'Artists do play God, to a certain extent. One invents out of dissatisfaction with the existing world. That dissatisfaction could be the greatest *hubris* of all, intentional blasphemy. But, if charged with blasphemy, I think an artist might insist that his own work be exhibited in his defence. If he could show, then, that the fragments he has created contain, and make manifest, order, pattern, a moral scheme, where before there was little or none, then at least it might be urged for him that he should be dealt with in mercy. But would you claim that there's any more order or pattern in your book than in this world? There's not, because you've taken your characters straight from life, you've made the plot a mere copy, or so you thought, of existing events. And what's your moral scheme? You've painted us all worse than we are, and I don't believe pardon will be extended you for that.'

Reduced at last to crudity, 'You must have a price,' she said. 'Everyone has a price. All you're really telling me is that I didn't offer you enough.'

'You've offered me too much. You've offered me—don't you understand?—far, far too much. You know how many bottles of whisky I could buy, with what you want to leave me? How much jewellery? How much' (I gestured around me) 'of this? I'd never have to paint again. I'd never be *able* to paint again. All I could do, all I need do, is die in the midst of my filthy riches.' With a yell of laughter, I said, 'And you wanted to buy me a man, too! My God, you want to make me frigid!'

Her breath was coming heavily, harshly, in gulps. 'If I'm not offering you enough, as from your sarcasm it seems you insinuate, tell me what I must add! What *is* your price?'

'I'm not in the market, Janice. I'm just not in the market.'

She refused to listen. 'The house!' she said triumphantly. 'I see, you want the house!'

'I don't know why your mind's so set on buying *me*,' I said. 'Why don't you make a bid for Celia?'

She took the suggestion seriously. 'She too, of course, would have the option of marrying Paul, if you allowed her to take it up. But that's not the same; it's not as attractive an idea. She would spend the money drably, drearily. You, on the other hand, would know very well how to enjoy it.'

'Is that a euphemistic way of saying I would undoubtedly squander it on myself in such a manner as to arouse your daughter's envy and increase her dislike?'

There was a trace of laughter in her eyes. 'No one would ever deny you style,' she said, trying, too late, to summon up her usual charm. 'Do you mind if I ask you who your parents were?'

'In the sense you mean, they were nobody, and now they're both dead I don't remember much about them, except that they were nice.'

'In the fairy-tales,' she jested, 'people like you always turn out to be the good king's daughter.'

'We're not in a fairy-tale. I don't think I've ever come across anything less like a fairy-tale in my life.'

'So,' she asked, 'you won't accept what I'm offering you?'

'If I wanted to I don't think I could, and not only because—something that seems to have escaped you—I'm *fond* of Paul. God, Janice, don't you see what you've done even yet? Listen—has anyone else read this book of yours?'

'No.'

'Are you sure?'

Her expression held alarm.

'Would it have been possible for anyone to gain access to it without your knowledge?'

But she still seemed not to understand. 'Why, anyone could have come in while I was asleep, but . . .'

'Could Jasmine have seen it?' I demanded.

'She typed it out for me.'

'I suppose you didn't know that as well as being Roddy's mistress she's also been trying to ingratiate herself with Paul? And that in case neither of those little plans comes off, she's found out something she could use for blackmailing Celia? Besides all of which, she's waiting to give the story of your death to her paper? But of course, she's irredeemably stupid, you think!'

For several seconds there was dead silence.

Needing air, I walked over to the window. 'Well,' I said, 'if you don't want to do what you can to make up to her for her rotten childhood, and you've given up the idea of securing yourself a niche in your horrid old heaven, you can still alter your will?'

There was an exclamation, and a crash. When I turned, Janice was lying back against the pillows, fighting for breath—the manuscript, and a glass of water, overturned on the floor beside her.

I said, 'I love you,' but she was already dead.

I picked up and smoothed out the wet manuscript, rang the housekeeper's bell, struggled with the door, and went, slowly, across the thick carpet of the antechamber towards the staircase.

5

In the cool, feminine room, whose elegance and subtlety was clearly designed to accommodate no more than two visitors at most, the gathering of so many ill-assorted persons became a breach of taste, of harmony, of decorum. Untidily obscured by redundant bodies, the mirrors' effect was lost. Someone (her daughter?) had substituted for the dead woman's single vase of white and amber roses a cut-glass bowl, hideously out of place, blossoming in blowsy red. Hovering, incongruous, in the air, intimations of Janice's presence were still, however, felt : its parody, or its wraith. Then as Jasmine brushed, looking for an ash-tray, past me, at once the reason was revealed : she wore a perfume that had belonged, characteristically, in very quintessence—musk, civet, mingling smoky spices—to her mother.

Sprawled in an arm-chair, silent, legs outstretched, Roddy showed the unkind marks of time. Art masters, music masters, are allowed a trace of the eccentric: his, greedily used, was the grossness with which, thus making his heaviness more obtrusive and pronounced, he chose viciously to slouch. How coarse, what a boor, he now was! Two places away from him, his sister appeared in contrast almost ethereally light, and Jasmine came back to her seat between them as if expressly to mediate between their polarities.

'If it isn't too mundane to mention,' I said, 'I feel absolutely starved.'

Jasmine's smile was for the first time almost friendly. 'Thank God I'm not the only one! There should be some chicken, I believe.'

Soon, on her return, we were all in shared guilt contentedly and ravenously eating.

'There was one thing I forgot to ask you, Anne,' said Paul, flicking from his lap, with regret, some crumbs. 'What happened to . . . ?'

'The other manuscript?' Jasmine put in.

'It's in my safe-keeping,' I said. 'It had a glass of water spilt over it, so I wanted to see that it came to no further harm.'

'The copyright must be worth something!' she objected.

'That,' I announced, addressing Paul, 'is precisely why I shall take good care of it until her literary executors claim it from me.'

Roddy began to look through the piles of records. Celia was already at work tidying up. The last crumpled rose-petals thrown away, in the absence of anything else to do she sat down, and said with a sisterly glance at Jasmine, 'The end of things is always so awful!'

'Even when it makes room for another start?' the girl asked.

Plaintive, with conscious heroism, Paul observed, 'If only I could face life as she faced death, I should be proud of my courage, and wouldn't think anyone had cause for regret. Anne—do you think this is the right moment to grin like that?'

'Sorry,' I said. 'Elegies, funerals, panegyrics, always make me laugh. It's a sort of nervous tic.'

'One you'd do well to control,' he said severely.

'I think Charles Lamb suffered from a similar affliction,' Celia murmured in appeasement.

Convulsed, 'Oh good,' I said, 'that makes it all right, doesn't it?'

Paul glared at me.

I pulled myself together. 'I wish I didn't hate people so much!'

'Even intelligent people?' asked Celia sympathetically.

'The only difference between the behaviour of intelligent and stupid people I've ever noticed is that the intelligent ones are nasty in a more interesting way.'

'Do you include yourself in that rather sweeping statement?' Paul inquired.

'Why not? No—to be serious, perhaps I don't exactly *hate* people—though I can't think of anyone I like, right now—but I certainly distrust most of them. I know, for instance, that *I* don't want war. I'm by no means certain that's true of anyone else in the world. In fact, it sometimes seems to me that I must be the only person at present in existence who wouldn't be willing in any circumstances to die on behalf of the Monroe Doctrine. Nor—to anticipate you, Paul—do I wish to die for Lenin, Engels, Trotsky or Karl Marx. Nor even Che Guevara.'

'Yes, but surely if you had to choose from among those philosophies ...'

'If I had to choose from among those *policies*, it wouldn't be surely, it would be with the utmost doubt. Our parents' generation were once given a choice between Hitler's Germany and Stalin's Russia, weren't they? Or so the story ran....'

'That's an original interpretation of the events leading up to the last war!'

'Oh, there were plenty of other stories. One other story was that Stalin's Russia was given a choice between the bloated capitalists of farther west, and those of Hitler's Germany. I don't think anyone liked making the choice then. And I should very much like to avoid being confronted with a similar one now.'

'All our parents' generation, or any other generation, could do was choose the lesser evil.'

'But I don't think anyone knew, or knows yet, which the lesser evil *was*! What they chose had nothing to do with evil; it had to do with strength.'

'Politics always has to do with strength, ultimately, but ...'

'Well, I wouldn't have wanted to take part in that game. I don't see why anyone *did*, unless, as I suspect, people basically like the idea of war.'

'What would you have done, then, in the same circumstances?' Paul asked.

'Opted out. Gone to prison, I suppose, if that was the alternative to supporting the war effort.'

'Very heroic, I'm sure,' he said. 'If everyone had thought in the same way ...'

'They didn't. And if they had, there wouldn't have been a war. There wouldn't have been a war, and people would be alive who aren't now.'

'Pacificism *leads* to war,' he declared.

'I've heard that slogan often enough, thank you. By pacificism I mean what the dictionary says, I mean "the doctrine that the abolition of war is both desirable and possible". How does *that* lead to war? I'm not talking about any kind of woolly-headed white-haired fellow-travelling, with banners, and processions, and telegrams to our allies in the Kremlin; and I'm not talking about laying my weapons down in the name of liberalism for the other side in the name of something else to pick them up, any more than I think it was sane for our parents' generation to disarm while the Japs and the Germans were busy with their fleets. My idea of pacificism is peace surrounded by arms.'

'Paradox upon paradox!'

'It's at least no more paradoxical than your bit of doublethink about pacificism's leading to war. I've always found concentration on the thought of solitary death extremely salutary. Well-adjusted people don't like the idea of death. They like to pretend as long as possible that it's something that only happens to someone else. When, as in war, they can't pretend *that* any longer, because their windows have just blown in, they pretend we all die together, in one big happy family. But we don't. We die alone, whether it's from some exquisite man-invented torture like nuclear radiation, or merely the result of one of Nobodaddy's more frivolous games, like cancer or yaws or the syph. Whether it's in a trench, choked with mud, or ringing a bell nobody answers in a hospital or a lonely room, whether it's here, or crawling around like brainless maggots in the ruins at Hiroshima, we die completely and utterly alone. Like her. Like Janice. Because you're not, I hope, going to tell me that even if one of us had been on each side, holding her hand, she'd have been any the less lonely, any the less alone?'

'Your concern for my wife is really very touching,' Paul said. 'Its pathos, though, is somewhat mitigated by the fact that you were in all probability the cause of her death, and also by your failure to attend her funeral today.'

'My concern isn't for your wife. It's for the living. I've never seen any point in weeping for the dead.'

'You don't deny, then, that your remarks on her novel are what caused her death?'

'In one sense we're all responsible. But you seem to be under a misapprehension, Paul. I didn't invent death. I didn't even invent heart disease. Somebody may be the Almighty, but it's not me.'

'Paul, accusations like that aren't really any help,' Celia interposed. 'We're all of us wrought up, and you certainly must be awfully tired. Let's give this subject a rest, for today.'

'I don't need rescuing, Celia,' I said. To Paul I added, 'Since I've never told you what opinion of the novel I expressed to Janice, and no one else was in the room, am I to deduce that Miss Donald was passing the key-hole during my last conversation with your wife?'

'You see what I mean?' Jasmine appealed to him. 'That's the kind of sniping I've had to put up with from her ever since we first met.'

Ignoring her, 'Am I under some kind of moral obligation to like your wife's entire literary output, Paul?' I asked.

'It might seem fittingly grateful from you,' he began, 'as the principal beneficiary under her will . . .'

'Oh, look!' said Celia. 'Can't this wait till some other time?'

'For us, it can, Celia,' I agreed. 'We have all the money we want and more than we need. Others aren't in the same case. I think Paul's tone is attributable to the fact that he believes I'm to inherit most of Janice's . . .'

'You don't inherit directly,' he conceded, 'but since I presume you're marrying Roddy...'

'Who says I'm marrying Roddy? Roddy, have you announced our engagement without so much as proposing to me?'

Sullen, Roddy shook his head.

'Then it will simplify matters no end if I declare right away that I am going to marry neither Roddy here, nor, Paul, you. Your move,' I said to Jasmine.

Once more Celia, a little pale, intervened. 'Anne, this is an important decision, you know.'

Roddy arose. He put down the two records he held, and reached towards the cut-glass bowl.

'Don't!' she suddenly cried.

The bowl was in smithereens. One after another, mirrors, mirrored windows, smashed. Paul caught up a paperweight, balanced it delicately in his right hand, and, just as Roddy finally advanced on Celia, smacked it into her brother's brow. Jasmine quickly thrust out her leg, and, Paul striking him again, ferociously, Roddy tumbled headlong across the record-player, bringing it down in a tangle of flex.

'Quite a team!' I said admiringly.

'You drove him to this!' said Celia. She looked at Jasmine, but she immediately added, 'All of you!'

It was Paul, whirling round from the telephone, who said what was in my mind. 'Whose brother is he, Celia? Whose responsibility?'

And, treacherously, I put the question she must already have been mentally answering: 'Didn't Cain say something rather like that, once?'

'... urgently, yes. Sedative? Yes, I think we have medication here, but would you hold on a moment?' He muffled the receiver against his chest. 'Jasmine?'

She nodded vehemently.

'Yes, we have a sedative ... yes, but there shouldn't be any delay. Thank you. Many thanks.' He put the telephone down. 'Really, Celia (can you find it then, sweet?), if you're going to make speeches about individual responsibility and Original Sin, you'll have to include yourself in your denunciations, won't you? I'd be prepared to discuss the proposition that we all drove him to it—even Janice herself—only you'll then have to allow that Roddy must share any guilt for what the rest of us have done.'

'Sorry,' she said, rubbing her temples. 'I don't really know what I meant.'

I leaped to the attack. 'Original Sin! Original stupidity is nearer the mark! Do you honestly consider yourself fairly accounted for by that simple-minded myth? Would any of you be so irresponsible, so childish, so *silly*, as to touch the one forbidden tree? Or respect the person who put it there? My God, I almost think you would!' Pausing, I tugged cigarettes and matches from my pocket. 'Look!' I struck a light. 'There you have it, the beautiful unworlding bomb, the new Yggdrasil, the forbidden New World tree!' Raising the match to my lips, I huffed, and, shuddering, the series of flame-moments flickered along its wood. 'There you had it, and in a moment—"phut!" went civilisation.'

With a small maddening laugh, Jasmine pointed.

I glanced again at the match. 'Hell—"phut!" it's sup*posed* to go!' I lit my cigarette. 'Next time, maybe.'

Celia shivered. Jasmine carefully cleared her syringe.

'Wouldn't intelligent people show contempt for a God like that?' I asked, shaking the flame out. 'Wouldn't you show your scorn for the prohibition by neither flouting nor respecting it? By simply not touching the fruit of that or any other tree in the whole garden?'

'We'd quietly starve, then, in the midst of Paradise?' Paul asked.

'That story always has seemed immoral to me,' Celia said in puzzlement. 'To forbid is to increase desire, isn't it? You don't need to do a course of practical psychology to know that if you tell a child there's one cupboard he mustn't touch he'll make straight for it once your back is turned. Whatever God one believes in, I think Anne's right to reject this primeval Bluebeard! Forbidden fruit may not taste the sweetest—I don't think for the normal person it ever does— but it smells and looks the sweetest of all.'

'Ah, Celia!' I said wearily. 'I've never met anyone with a talent like yours for missing the point.'

'I wouldn't claim to be an expert on the normal,' said Paul

thoughtfully, 'but I don't think I'd agree with all that. Take the forbidden sexual relationships, for instance—sexual taboos. Would you say incest smelled very sweet, Celia? Incest between a sister and a brother, say?'

Jasmine paused in administering the injection, then silently and efficiently plunged the needle down.

'It's a matter of convention,' I said.

'Yes: in some societies we regard as comparatively primitive many more relationships are *verboten* than we find it necessary to ban in ours. But the very fact that so few conjunctions are regarded as incestuous in our world might make the guilt of those who did transgress appear especially heinous, mightn't it? To, I mean, themselves? If there was only one case recognised as incest, that of brother and sister, then according to your argument, Celia, it would exert extreme fascination, wouldn't it? On, of course, those attracted to that particular species of tree.'

'What is it you're really saying?' Celia asked. She was anxious and fluttered, but her manner was gentle, it besought.

'Why, nothing,' he said. 'For in fact many other cases of incest are recognised and occur.'

'Had you,' I asked, 'ever considered the case of a father and a daughter? With the daughter perhaps below the age of consent?'

Paul swallowed. 'No. No, I hadn't considered that.' He steadied himself, evidently determined not to allow reason to have any influence on his decision. 'As you say . . . there's the case of a man and his daughter; as well as,' he continued, suddenly venomous, 'a man and his son. Your father was interested in homosexuality, wasn't he, Celia? I would awfully have liked to discuss this subject in detail with him.'

Celia had gone white. 'If there's some accusation you want to make, Paul, I think you'd better make it in plainer words.'

He regarded her with melancholy tenderness. 'I have no accusations. I just feel there are people I would rather make my idol than my wife; and having made anyone my idol, my own private saint, I don't want to learn she has a murky past, or know anything about the circumstances causing it.'

'How very male!' I observed.

'All our lives seem to have become public,' he apologised, dulcet again. 'That's why I ...'

Celia's smile was natural and kind. 'I understand.'

Extinguishing my cigarette, I crossed to the windows and flung them up, one after another, to let out the stale smoke.

'I don't understand,' I said. 'I'll never understand.'

Celia said softly, 'Don't be so upset, Anne. None of this matters any more to me. What haunts me is that there's still no fountain in our *patio* in Guatemala.'

Jasmine and I exchanged a long, eloquent look.

'Do you mean to say,' I asked Celia incredulously, 'that after all this you still believe in God and Destiny and Grace?'

Jasmine laughed again, and bent to plant a kiss on Roddy's oblivious head; then, still laughing, she covered him with a blanket, and put out her hand to Paul.

The sunlight touching her hair to a golden nimbus, Celia responded with a smile that, however sad, expressed utter peace, 'I think I still believe in people, Anne, and believe that people can be helped.'

Epilogue

Not in Utopia,—subterranean fields,—
Or some secreted island, Heaven knows where!
But in the very world, which is the world
Of all of us,—the place where, in the end,
We find our happiness, or not at all!

William Wordsworth, *The Prelude*, XI. 140–45

Absorbed, silent, Anne stood before the easel, mixing on her palette another shade of green. Testing the bright pigment on the back of her hand, then on a piece of rag, at last she swept the thickest brush across the canvas, satisfied.

Steps sounded rapidly on the staircase. Paul pushed open the door.

The brush trembled. With an exclamation she groped for the palette knife and lifted with it a streak of paint.

'Sorry, did I startle you? You don't mind if I come in?'

'Not at all, do!'

Awkwardly he put out his hand.

'You're going now, then?' she asked, abandoning her work. 'You've got everything?'

He nodded. They came spontaneously together and embraced.

She freed herself. 'No, we shouldn't do things that are meaningless. You don't belong to me any more. Or rather, you never did; nor I to you. So what would be the point? Have some whisky with me.'

He refused. 'Just because we wake up,' he said pleadingly, 'it doesn't mean the whole of yesterday was a dream?'

'The whole of today and tomorrow could be a dream, whether or not any of us awake from it!'

'Anne, answer me something?' he asked. 'Haven't you honestly had any happiness with me?'

'With you I've had' (she touched his face very gently, but without looking into his eyes) 'something that's precious to me.'

'You're not answering my question.'

'I don't'—her voice broke—'I don't know the answer to any questions. Why *should* I? Why *should* I?'

'You're not crying, Anne?'

Her face was hidden from him.

'Anne, you won't go on drinking too much?'

'I shouldn't imagine so,' she said in a smothered tone. 'Not now I've started working again.'

'Promise me?'

'Paul, will you for heaven's sake not meddle in my affairs! I'll promise nothing. Promises have on me completely the wrong psychological effect.'

They both listened. The ringing sounded again, and in relief she went towards the door.

Returning, now calm, 'Wrong number, as usual!' she said.

'You'll stay in this house, won't you? I'd like you to have that.'

She laughed. 'I don't think Jasmine would. The money, don't forget, is in her name!'

'You mustn't think so badly of her.'

'You're not critical enough,' she casually rejoined, undisguised amusement on her face.

Poisonous, lethal, with full intent, 'You're *too* critical,' he said.

When the blow had fallen, she sought, finding herself still whole, a riposte equal to it in force, in sharpness, and in its power to hurt. The realisation came to her that Paul did not know what Roddy, Celia, and she herself knew: that Jasmine was the daughter of his wife; and the temptation to use the

236

information to prevent his marriage with the girl was suddenly so strong that Anne took a step backwards, nearly
knocking her canvas to the floor. Then, the so-much-wanted
victory surrendered even as she wore it, triumphantly, on her
face, with a laugh she said, reflecting that here lay her rival's
chief, though negative, attraction: 'Jasmine isn't *that*! I don't
think badly of her,' she added. 'By the way, what's going to
happen to Roddy?'

'He needs treatment; we can't make definite plans until we
see the results. But certainly it would seem advisable to get
him out of his present job. Perhaps there'd be less strain on
him if he was given the opportunity and the leisure to compose; at any rate, that's what we think. He's always liked the
idea of living on a farm—I don't know that we'd enjoy having
him with us permanently, and Celia will want some say in
the matter, but when she starts her social work in Guatemala
he could come to us for holidays, at least.'

'Oh, Paul!' she said with delight. 'You're going to have your
farm?'

His face broke into an answering smile.

'I'm so pleased!' But as if in any shared emotion she saw
danger, she reverted at once to her usual mockery. 'So for the
rest of your life you'll be mixed up with the whole pack of
them? Men never learn!'

This time he refused to quarrel. 'Will you stay, then, Anne?'

'No—very nice of you, but it would be enough if I could
just stop on a few days to finish this picture. The light here's
good.'

'And afterwards?'

'Afterwards would be my business, wouldn't it?'

The colour came to his cheeks. 'I beg your pardon.'

Her own face suddenly red, she put down her glass and
looked directly at him. 'I'm sorry. I didn't mean that.'

'I know. I only wondered if perhaps there was any chance
of that . . . card coming, at long last.'

'Card?'

'The one from Takla Makan.'

Close to tears, yet with the old half-mischievous, half-rueful
grin, 'You've *not* been waiting for Alan's card all this time,
Paul?'

237

He mumbled, 'I thought maybe *you* had.'

The expedient lie failed her.

'You always liked him, didn't you?'

Not trusting herself to speak, she nodded.

He said simply, 'I've never been much good for you.'

A choking sound came from her.

'Don't,' he said, putting his arm around her shoulders.

'It's—it's always been quite the other way! I've always somehow had the effect of discouraging you from work—you've never . . .'

'Hush!' he said, squeezing her to him. 'Don't cut it all to bits! Whatever the word is that you can't find for what you've had with me, I've experienced the same with you!'

She made a great effort. 'One thing I want to make clear to you, Paul: even if Alan does come back, I don't think I'll be marrying him. Some women seem to be predestined wives; others, like me, are best at dealing with the parts of a man that marriage ignores or tries to kill. Oh, I won't lie to you—it's possible, of course, that if he proposed to me again I'd find the easier answer "Yes". But I think not.'

'There are plenty of men more imaginative than I,' he said awkwardly, 'and Alan sounds like one of them. Maybe quite soon you'll . . .'

'It's not that. Not hurt pride.'

His lips touched once the crown of her hair; he released her; they both moved finally away.

'Maudlin!' she muttered, rubbing at her cheeks with the piece of rag, and energetically snatched up the brush. 'Everyone's got what they want, then, more or less,' she murmured.

'Everyone except you,' Paul replied.

'Oh, I . . . I've never known what it is I want,' she said absently; her thoughts had already left him.

He wrinkled his nose. 'I shall always associate this room with the smell of paint! But there's something else—what is it?' He came over and looked at her canvas. 'I do believe you're using oil!'

Still absently, she nodded.

From her accounts of it he recognised the bleakness, the black boughs before him, the single path that led inexorably into a solitude of green.

'This is the garden?' he inquired, surprised. 'You used to say it would be your last picture!'

Becoming momentarily aware of him, Anne smiled. 'I think it's really my first.'

'As well?' Paul asked. 'Or instead?'

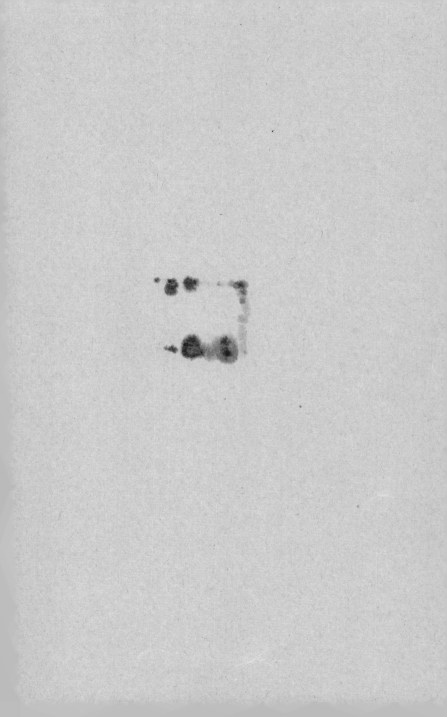

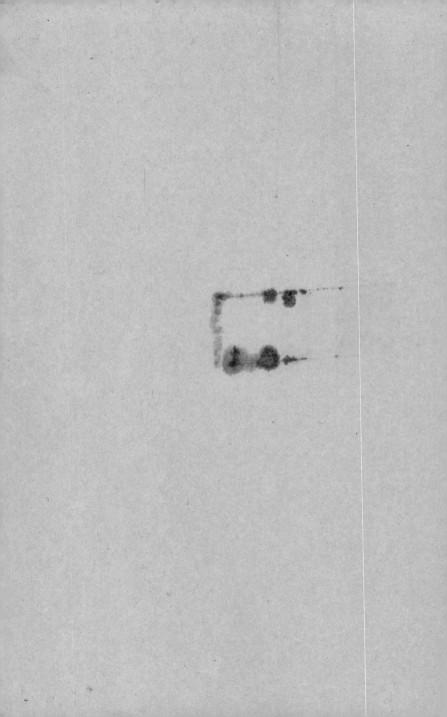